Who Would Have Dreamed

A NOVEL OF MIRACLES

SHARON LEE FOLEY

ISBN
978-1-958690-95-6 (Paperback)
978-1-958690-96-3 (eBook)

Table of Contents

Chapter 1

"You'd think she was the only widow in the world," Fran said, scowling out the front window as her neighbor backed her car down her driveway and into the street.

"Oh, leave her be," Milly said as she polished her sister's fine silver at the dining room table. "She doesn't hurt anyone by driving out. . . there." Milly was the superstitious type. Milly avoided talking about death or cemeteries or diseases that could lie in wait until you acknowledged them, and then—poof—there they were, attacking you, growing, and actually feeding off you. She'd seen it happen.

"She doesn't hurt anyone, you say," Fran snapped. "She only hurts herself, is all. Going out there almost every single day for what—two months now?"

Milly glanced up from her work and shook her head at the air. "Has it been that long?" It really did just seem like a few days ago that the paramedics had carried Bill out on that stretcher. Poor, poor Eleanor.

"Well, I think it's high time we call her daughter."

"Oh, Fran, let's not. It's really none of our business."

"Says who? I've lived across the street from Eleanor for thirty-five years. What kind of a neighbor would I be if I just look away from things like this?" Fran left her post at the window to go to the phone. "Besides, how else will her daughter know? She ain't been back since she and her boyfriend ... if you can call a man in his late forties a boy. Maybe he's even fifty, who knows with that Trashy Trish! Anyway, they haven't been back since the funeral, and then they stayed just long enough to pilfer through Bill's things. . ."

"Fran, please, that's so unkind."

"Well, excuse me for telling the truth."

"Maybe," Milly said, screwing the cap tightly on the polish can so she wouldn't accidentally bump it over. "Maybe we should just go and talk to Eleanor. Try to get her involved in things. Make an effort to invite her over more often."

Fran grunted as she bent to get the address book from the shelf under the phone table. "And we haven't? Wasn't it us who invited her over just last Tuesday when you'd gone berserk making enough chicken and biscuits to feed the whole town? And then, when we were thoughtful enough to invite her, did she come? No. No, she did not. 'Thank you, but I've already eaten,' she said."

"All I'm saying . . .," Milly began, but Fran was already dialing.

⸻⁓ꞁꞁꞁo₀℮ⳡⲟⲅℯⲟ℃ꞁꞁꞁ⸻

Eleanor parked in her usual place. She glanced in the rearview mirror and gave her hair a quick pat, then she got out and went around to the trunk. She got out her canvas and paint box. Her heart trembled with excitement as it always did when she got here. Who would have dreamed?

Daniel appeared at the door of his studio, tall and willowy and tan under his silver hair. Her heart leaped at the sight of him. Oh yes, who could have dreamed?

"The light is perfect now," Daniel said, walking out to take the paint box from her. He shrugged and smiled. "You must have brought the sunshine with you."

Eleanor blushed. No one in real life talked like Daniel. But then he was an artist—a handsome hero from some romantic novel, who had moved to this backward small corner of the world to discover. .. her.

For that was what had happened. Fate had brought Daniel to Gilmont to save her.

It had been the first of April—spring, how appropriate—when she had first met Daniel. She had escaped the dreariness of a winter house to wander outside and breathe in the first clean promise of spring. She'd walked down her street and across the town common. Fresh blades of green grass were just starting to poke through the dead brown mat of last year. Tender daffodils trembled in the warm breeze. You could, if you tried, smell the last of the snow melting in the shadows of the distant woods.

Eleanor walked down the main street, pausing to study the displays in the shop windows—light sweaters in fresh colors of peach and yellow, skirts and tops as skimpy and sequined as fairy clothes, books to be read, lotions to buy, gardening tools, and a sale on tenderloin. Old friends nodded. Children skipped beside their mothers. She should have been prepared for something wonderful to happen. But she hadn't been. In fact, when she had paused in front of Daniel's tiny art-supply store to admire a painting in the window, and he had actually come to the door and had spoken to her, she was totally caught off guard. She had been safe and content in her own thoughts when suddenly he appeared and told her he gave painting lessons, if she was interested.

"Oh, no. No. I could never," Eleanor had said, flashing a grateful smile but still shaking her head.

"You've studied that painting for a while."

Eleanor had looked back at it. It was a road curving out of sight under a canopy of autumn trees. Dusty light streamed through the branches onto the leaf-scattered road. It gave her a soft, lonely feeling, not of anticipation or hope of what was around the corner, but rather a quiet resignation of this moment in her life. She sighed.

"I can teach you."

Eleanor glanced back at this sincere, handsome man. He wouldn't understand she wasn't studying it to replicate it. She was standing on that road, alone, her summers behind her.

"Tell you what," he had said, "I'll give you the first lesson free."

"No, I couldn't possibly do that."

"Do what? Try?"

"No, I mean, impose. Take up your time."

"It's mine to give," he had said, and then he had winked at her. "Here we are, fate and me inviting you in. It could be just what you're looking for."

And so after much protesting and denying that she had any talent, he had somehow wheedled a commitment out of her. She would come on Tuesday. He closed the shop on Tuesdays at five o'clock to give lessons. She wouldn't have to buy anything on the first lesson— just try it and see how she liked it.

Eleanor didn't notice anything on her walk back home. She hurried past the shops and people, heavy with dread that she had made the promise. For he had actually asked her to promise. Like she was twelve! But somehow she had done it. Though it's not like he could come to her house and get her if she broke her promise. So what was it? Why did the thought of starting painting classes feel so frightening? It was more than the disappointment of failing, more than arguing with Bill about the cost. It was . . . suddenly realizing that she wanted something like that so badly. Something for herself, about herself, something beautiful drawn from the constant ache of loneliness inside her. At that moment, she could have easily wept from the fear of hoping.

Tuesday morning she had wandered through her rooms, studying the pictures on the walls, the wallpaper designs, and the streams of light shining through the budded branches of the maple tree onto her wood floor. She tried to see—really, actually see—with an artist's eye the ordinary things one often overlooked. She needed to discover something to take with her to class, something Daniel would notice and nod about. But at four forty-three when she closed her front door behind her, she was as insecure as the day she had promised to try.

When she got to Daniel's shop, there were already five other women there. Three Eleanor knew. One was Doris Hartsborne. Doris had been two years ahead of Eleanor throughout their school years. Doris was one of those who were into everything—cheerleading, student council, yearbook committee—anything that drew attention to her. At least that was the way Eleanor had felt about her. Eleanor was a little disappointed to see Doris in the class.

Pauline Miller was there. No one could help but like Pauline. She was soft in manner and dress. Not exactly timid, but rather gentle. Certainly, the opposite of Doris!

Ruthie Barton was the other woman Eleanor knew. Ruthie was the good-time girl. She was no beauty or brain, but when she walked into a room, everyone found themselves smiling. Ruthie had been through a lot of drama in her life that would have crippled other women, but she kept on rolling with a sense of humor that could almost make you envy her for how funny her tragedies were.

The other two women in the class were young. One was maybe right out of high school, maybe not, one of those strange, dark, gothic-looking too-thin girls. And the other was, Eleanor guessed, in her mid-thirties though it was hard to tell with the way she slouched and didn't try to make the effort to keep her appearance up.

At five o'clock Daniel turned the Open sign around in the door window.

"Store is closed," Ruthie said. "Class is now open. Ladies, start your engines."

Daniel smiled at her, introduced Eleanor, and asked everyone to set up their easels.

"I think this easel will work for you," Daniel said, leading Eleanor to one that he had set up. "Do you have something in mind you want to begin with?"

Eleanor shrugged. "I thought you would be teaching, you know, whatever you teach."

"I don't teach you to paint like me. I teach you to paint like you."

"I see," Eleanor said.

"Scary, heh?" Ruthie said. "Imagine what mine must be like."

"You can start by copying the painting in the window," Daniel offered.

Eleanor nodded. Yes, sure, that would be all right. Not too many colors, no people, not a lot of sky. She didn't think she could paint air and clouds.

Daniel went to take the road painting out of the window.

"He really is great," Pauline whispered. "He just seems to know what suits us. My first painting was of flowers, pansies really, and it was awful." She smiled at the memory of it. "Then he had me try this abstract. It doesn't make sense to me, but I like it. I just like the shapes and colors, and I think when I get done copying this one, I want to try one on my own."

Eleanor stepped around Pauline's easel. It was totally not what Eleanor had expected. The colors were too intense, basic really, and the shapes were simple and sharp. What could Pauline, of all people, love about that?

"I know." Pauline giggled. "But I can't wait to get here and paint it."

"Daniel, Daniel, could you stop here a minute? Just a minute," Doris said as Daniel was passing by her.

"Oh god," Ruthie said, rolling her eyes. "Drama Queen probably can't open her paint with those daggers she glues on for nails."

When everyone was set up and ready, Daniel stood with his back to them and quickly drew an egg shape on a piece of heavy paper. He then explained his color choices, his brush size, the angle of light he wanted on the egg, and how to contour the shading to make it appear dimensional. He finished with a few quick speckles on the egg, and everyone stood and just admired, for the first time in their lives, the simple beauty of an egg.

Eleanor watched Daniel and knew that if she didn't paint a stroke, she would take something away with her. For even if she discovered that she really didn't have any talent, in one brief moment, he had taught her to, at least, see. He was amazing.

Eleanor had returned each week for the four months before Bill died. She and Bill had exchanged differing opinions about the art classes. Yes, they were an extra expense and just when he was getting ready to retire. Yes, she could get books at the library and practice the basics herself before they invested in classes. Yes, she would admit it would be an investment without a return; she wasn't pretending that she would ever be good enough to sell her work. Yes, she could get a part-time job if she just wanted to get out of the house. Yes. Yes. Yes. And yet he would have to divorce her to stop her.

"It's not so much the cost," Bill had finally confided. "It's just that you've changed since you started going there. Always reading those art books, drifting off when I'm trying to talk to you. And . . . and though I'm not saying it's a bad thing, you've started wearing perfume and rubbing lotion everywhere. Your elbows and heels. Who looks at your heels anyway?"

"I do," she had retorted.

"Humph," Bill had said. And that was where they had stood on the subject until the day he had suffered the fatal heart attack and left her.

She had, of course, stopped going to the classes after Bill's death. But when the shock and decisions and sympathy were over, and Trish had gone back to Florida, she found herself alone wandering around the empty rooms. She was sitting on the back porch one evening, staring out at the garden Bill had planted in the corner of the yard, and wondering if she had the heart to harvest it when her doorbell rang. Assuming it was Milly from across the street, sneaking over while Fran napped, Eleanor was surprised to see Daniel.

"How are you doing?" he asked when she opened the screen door for him.

She smiled and shrugged.

He nodded, understanding, and followed her into her living room.

"I was just having some ice tea. Would you like some?" Eleanor asked.

"Actually," he said, holding out a brown bag shaped like a wine bottle, "I found this great bottle of prosecco I'd been saving for an occasion. Do you drink wine?"

She smiled. "I've been known to sip a glass."

"Great," he said.

So Daniel opened the wine, and they sat in the kitchen, her space, and they talked. He told her about his wife and how he had coped, or not coped, after her death. His wife had been an artist also, and they had owned their own shop in Boston when she was diagnosed with breast cancer. She had fought with courage and hope, hiding her full suffering from him as long as she could until there was no more hope, hiding, or courage left.

There was physical pain in Eleanor's heart as she listened to him. As tragic as it was to have lost Bill so unexpectedly, she was grateful now that she hadn't had to sit helplessly by and watch him suffer so painfully minute by minute until he just gave up. Bill was a proud man; he would have hated to wither in body and courage. She'd only seen fear in Bill's eyes once, and that had been enough.

When they finished the wine and were resting from their grief, Daniel had asked her if she would be coming back to class.

"Bill never approved of me taking those classes."

"And yet you did."

She nodded.

"I'm assuming he came to understand."

"I can't say that he understood, only that he came to accept it was something I needed to do. After a while we stopped discussing it. We just accepted that it was something we would silently disagree about."

"All marriages have those issues," Daniel said, and for the first time Eleanor felt better about the disappointment of Bill's refusing to discuss it.

"What did he think of your finished painting?"

"He never saw it. I put it in the back of a closet."

"It wasn't that bad," Daniel said and smiled.

"I just couldn't risk it."

"Well, can you risk it now?"

Eleanor frowned.

"The class has asked me to open the shop one night for an art exhibit of their work."

"Really?"

"Actually, it was Doris's idea, but I think the rest are excited about it now."

Eleanor shook her head. "I'm not ready. I don't even have my second painting finished."

"That's why I stopped by," he said. "I want to help you catch up. If you aren't up to coming back to classes, I thought you could come out to my house and work there. I have a small studio where I do my own work."

"No. No, I couldn't possibly . . . you can't be serious?"

"I'm always serious."

"What would people think?"

"Is that your only reason?"

Eleanor thought then smiled. "Yes. How pitiful."

Daniel stood up. "The shop number also rings at my house," he said.

So Eleanor rang that number and found her way to his house nearly every day after he closed his shop. It was wonderful. It was like she was now someone who wasn't even her. When she wasn't there, she was thinking of being there. Daniel had been a perfect gentlemen; she only stayed her hour of paid class time, and yet she felt like she was somehow hiding inside someone else. It was like she could almost watch herself from a distance as she pretended to be this artist. Certainly, she, the real Eleanor Sisson, was not going to a real artist's studio and working on her own painting. Certainly, the real artist wasn't treating her as though it was his delight to have her there. Who was this woman whom Daniel had become so comfortable with and who, so out of character for her, may have, on occasion, brazenly flirted back? It couldn't really be her who would bring Daniel from his work when he noticed her tap the brush handle against her lips and frown at her canvas. But Daniel would leave his work and stroll over to her. More color here. Shadow isn't black. Work from the distance into the light.

And yet it was. Daniel had given her a life she would have never dared hope for from the first day she'd met him to this moment when he was carrying her paints into his studio. Who would have dreamed?

"I'm telling you, your mother is not doing well, and all you can say is that it is to be expected," Fran said, rolling her eyes so Milly could attest to her disgust. "Thank the Lord, I never had any children, if this is how much a mother can expect from one."

Milly sucked in her breath. She could live to be a million and still never understand how outrageous her sister could be. It was like people didn't even have feelings the way Fran treated them.

"Oh, I don't know. Maybe you could think just once about the woman who gave up everything to spoil you rotten, and come home and check on her. Maybe that is all it would take. It's not like you're really working there." Fran put her hand over the phone and whispered to Milly that being a limo driver for a hotel was nothing that anyone should be bragging about.

"Get like that if you want, but when something happens to that good woman, it will be on your conscience, not mine. All I can do is put the responsibility where it belongs. It's not like I'm going to inherit anything if she dies from a broken heart."

"Oh, Fran," Milly said.

"Yes, by all means, go. Don't leave those high and mighty rich people waiting for a limousine ride to some sleazy booze joint. Heaven forbid, you should be responsible for disappointing them."

Milly dropped the spoon she was polishing.

"I'll call you if I see an ambulance over there," Fran said and slammed the phone down in its cradle. "And some folks still don't believe in the seed of the devil."

Milly crossed herself. She wasn't Catholic, but it never hurt.

Eleanor pulled her car up to the garage and got out. She'd left her canvas and paints at Daniel's studio. She had gotten a lot of work done today, and Daniel suggested she let her canvas dry more before she moved it. He was certain it would be ready for the show in a couple of weeks. Eleanor felt a thrill at the thought of her painting being locked inside Daniel's studio with all his paints and canvases and his art . . . the essence of his vision and feelings. The things that meant the most to him. It felt intimate somehow.

Eleanor started toward the back steps when the redness of a tomato hanging from a vine in Bill's garden caught her eye. She sat her purse on the stoop and walked toward it. My goodness, there are so many. How had she not noticed? She went to the shed and got a basket and began picking, pausing to appreciate the red, red color, how the early evening light made them softer than the shiny toughness of the midday sun, and how she had to turn them in her hand to twist them free from the hairy . . . what green? Sea green? No. Yellow green? Closer but not right.

"Eleanor."

A voice behind her startled Eleanor, and she jumped, creasing the vine and crushing the tomato.

"Good gracious," Fran said, "aren't you the jumpy one? Guilty conscience?"

Eleanor dropped the tomato and shook the juice from her hand. She forced a smile for Fran.

"I've been noticing your garden," Fran said. "Pity to let it go to waste."

"Yes, I agree. I'm afraid I haven't been as diligent as I should be."

"It's not like you have a lot else to do," Fran said.

"Well, as you can see, I'm living up to my responsibilities now."

Fran nodded. "Bill always planted a good garden."

"Yes, yes, he did."

"Will you be canning all this? I mean, for just you?"

Eleanor looked at Fran, at Bill's garden, and at the empty house. The sun was just setting behind the treetops. How could she bear all this without the diversion of Daniel? She breathed the barest whisper of his name.

"What? What was that?"

Eleanor turned back to Fran. "No, of course, I can't use all this for just myself. Please help me. Take some. As much as you want."

Fran smiled, pleased about the tomatoes, then got to the reason she had come across the street. "I've noticed you leaving every day at the same time."

"Is that so?"

"It's not a good idea, not healthy, to go to the cemetery every day. When Philip was killed in that accident at the mill, I knew right away the best thing I could do for myself was to just get on with it. Nothing I could do or suffer could bring him back. I visit his grave on Memorial Day when we all go to the cemetery, but I don't let myself become a prisoner to my loss."

Eleanor just looked at her.

"I'm not saying it was easy. Just what we have to do."

"I see."

"Good. Good, then. Now, I'll just go get Milly and be back to help you before the sun goes down." Fran started to walk away then stopped and smacked at a mosquito on her arm. "Best get some bug repellant too," she muttered.

Eleanor took the few tomatoes she had picked and retrieved her purse from the steps and went into her house. How could one person suck all the color out of your life? Eleanor sat her purse on the table and walked into the living room. The answering machine was blinking. She frowned and went over to punch the Play button.

"Mom, just checking in. You okay? I'm working tonight. Call me tomorrow if you need me."

Eleanor erased it. Maybe someone's mother had been killed in front of Trish, and it had reminded Trish for a moment that she actually had a mother of her own.

Of course, Doris knew the moment Daniel's shop first opened. Actually, she'd known when the lease was signed. A handsome artist from Boston, trying to bring art to Gilmont was not everyday news. So naturally, she went right to check it out.

At the first sign of activity in the shop, Doris had tapped on the window and smiled in at Daniel. He was a good-looking man. Maybe hanging out at the shop would get that slug of a husband of hers to feel a little nervous. Ha!

Daniel had opened the door and greeted her, and she had introduced herself to him.

"How on earth did you ever decide to set up shop in our little town?" she'd asked, smiling so he could not miss her great dimples and straight white teeth. Her blond hair was freshly colored, so she was confident she didn't look near her age. Though the gray of his hair and fine crow's-feet at his eyes probably didn't put him far from her sixty years. Still, she totally believed that sixty today was really like being forty.

Daniel hadn't invited her in—things were too unorganized— but he had stood patiently at the door and answered her questions. She'd left feeling like she had made a great impression on him as to the quality of people here in Gilmont. Now if the rest of the town could only clean up their acts. Some days she felt a little depressed to have spent her whole life here.

Doris had checked on Daniel's progress daily. She offered him advice when it was obvious he needed it and even brought some potential customers around to meet him. He'd only been in town two weeks when she felt that they were old friends. She was certain he felt that way too.

Being one of the self-appointed town leaders, she was, of course, obligated to host his grand-opening gala. Daniel had protested—it was way too much to ask—but she had just pooh-poohed his protests away. He obviously couldn't understand the full responsibilities of her popularity and influence in the town.

So on the day the doors were to open, Doris and her barrage of ladies-in-waiting converged on the little art shop with linen tablecloths, candelabras, silver bowls, and platters of hors d'oeuvres and— don't be absurd—of course, fresh flowers. Who could do it better in Boston? Signs had been posted in the other stores' windows, and without question, anyone who knew Doris knew that they had better come and welcome the new artist.

Daniel had stood in the open doorway as streams of townspeople wandered in and out of his shop. Most of them just drank a little punch and ate as much as politely possible but didn't know quite what to say to the host. Still, the evening had been a great success by Doris's standards. She and her crew had gathered their empty dishes and candlestick nubs and left the store without a sign they had ever been there. Daniel had to be impressed with the efficiency of that!

Doris had driven away, swollen with good feelings and pride, certain she had made a difference in Daniel's success. It wasn't until she turned into the driveway of her grand Victorian house that it occurred to her that Frederick had not attended the opening. Her own husband hadn't even had respect enough for her to show his selfish old face for five minutes. God, how she hated that man!

Doris sat in the car with the headlights on, the radio playing some sad love song, her good feelings melting into a puddle of disappointment at her feet. How could he, after forty years of marriage, keep doing this to her? Every man in town had dreamed of marrying her, but no, no, she had to have Frederick—the one guy who had never seemed that impressed with her. Why? Why had she chosen him? Was it some kind of mental illness? Or a curse? Had someone been so jealous of her that they had put a curse on her to love the only man who wouldn't love her back?

Doris sat there forever, and not once did a curtain stir or the porch light come on to welcome her home. Not once did it occur to Frederick to come out to help her carry in her things. He was in there. He was sitting his arrogant old self in front of the stupid TV or was holed up in his office without a clue if she was even in the house or not. Maybe he never even knew she'd gone out.

Finally, Doris turned off the lights and the car and got out. There was no bounce of success as she went up the broad steps to her front door. There was no sound as she opened the leaded glass door, no greeting as she put her purse on the foyer table and headed to the kitchen. She snapped on the kitchen light. Well, at least he wasn't lying somewhere, withering away from starvation. Doris walked over to the island and surveyed the debris of his evening meal. He didn't have to adore her the way everyone else did, but at least he could show her some respect, some thoughtfulness. Was that too much to ask in return for forty years of being loved and taken care of?

Normally, Doris would not have gone to bed with the kitchen looking like a pigsty, but tonight she just didn't have it in her to touch a thing. Tonight she had needed Frederick to show up at her event and meet Daniel and glance over what a beautiful job she had done. She needed him to be proud of her. It was like the time she was crowned queen of the senior prom; he had hardly acknowledged it. Everyone else was fawning all over her, but Frederick had just slipped outside to one of his buddies' cars to sneak some whiskey, and she hadn't seen him again until she had to drive him home. She was such an idiot!

Doris was still awake, though she was pretending not to be, when Frederick finally came into the bedroom. He walked through the bedroom and in to the bathroom. She was sixty, and still a tear could escape. She had to do something. If she didn't, she would end up killing him. She would. She'd kill him dead as a doornail. She'd poison him and stand there and watch him gasp for his last breath, and she'd say, "Well, do you see me now? Do I have any importance in your life now?" Or she would shoot him. Take one of his prize pistols out of its velvet box and point it at him. Point it square at his black hole of a heart and smile. "This is far more sudden than the death I've felt living with you," she'd say, and he'd probably beg for another chance, beg her to let him try to be a good husband like she deserved. He'd probably tell her how he'd always adored her but didn't know how to show it. But she'd still pull the trigger. She deserved his remorse and death.

Frederick opened the bathroom door and turned off the light. Doris could hear him making his way to his side of the bed in the darkness. She wished she'd dropped something sharp on the floor. She felt the bed sag a little as he sat down, then lay down. Then Frederick did something totally... unforgivable. He leaned over and lightly kissed her shoulder.

—⁓⁓⁓⁓⁓⁓⁓⁓⁓—

Pauline had once thought of taking art classes. She'd even gone so far—before the kids, of course—as to buy some oils and brushes. She had a couple of canvases hidden up in the attic. She wasn't proud of them. Guess she mostly kept them as a reminder of when she had a life of her own. Dreams and thoughts of her own. Not that Pauline was complaining. She loved her children and wouldn't have wanted her life to be any different from how it had turned out. But still, contentment aside, she had always wanted to paint. So when she saw the sign in the grocery store about the opening of an art shop that offered painting classes, her secret self rejoiced. She didn't say anything to Tim right away; she'd just squirrel away a little money to pay for the classes first, and then she'd tell him. Tim was an easygoing guy who wouldn't say no, but she knew he couldn't help but fuss and worry about the budget. Marry an accountant and what did you expect?

Pauline found it was actually easy to skimp a little here and there. So okay, hamburger twice a week, and didn't the kids tell her they loved the smell of the store brand of shampoo? Certainly, Jeffrey's pajamas could last him another winter. He could wear socks if his ankles were cold. Yes, where there was a will, there was a way. And she had the will to paint.

Pauline's plan seemed flawless until . . . Jennifer got a cavity. True, it was a baby tooth, but still the motherly thing to do would be to get it filled so Jennifer wouldn't get a toothache by ignoring it or have it pulled and risk her teeth shifting and having her new teeth coming in crooked. Braces were much more expensive than a filling. So there went her painting-class money.

Still, with or without the classes, she could still go to the art store and browse around. The smell of oils and turpentine and the dust of pastel chalks satisfied something in her. She'd pick up the instruction books and leaf through them, and then she'd put them back. She'd stand in front of a partially done canvas and imagine how she would finish it. Art was in her even if it couldn't get out. Thank God for this store.

So it was an unbelievable surprise to her when Daniel approached her one day as she was concentrating on the array of fine-pointed brushes displayed like art itself and asked her if she'd like to take lessons.

"Oh, who wouldn't?" she'd replied, and he'd smiled at her. She liked Daniel; he was not like the folks around here. Like her, there was a gentleness about him, a patience and appreciation for things other than work. She liked to believe she saw more than what was obvious and before her. Somewhere inside her was something different that others couldn't see.

"I'm starting classes on Tuesday," he'd said, and she had blushed and replied that she'd love nothing more, but she had two kids, and their needs had to come before hers. "Someday," she said.

"I couldn't possibly deprive your children of their needs, but on the other hand, I can't, in good conscience, see a potential artist lost but for the mere lack of money."

"*Mere* must hold a different meaning in your world," she had said.

"Tell you what, I could use help in the store on . . . what days are you available?"

Pauline had to admit that she had blushed to think this man, a virtual stranger, was offering her a job, and he was doing it because it was so obvious she wanted to paint. In the space of a minute, he had cut to the heart of her.

"That's very nice of you," she'd said.

"But? What? You can't spare a few hours a week for art?"

"Well, yes, of course, I can. It's just that, well, you don't even know me. How can you make an offer when you have never even spoken to me before?"

"True, I may not have spoken to you, but that doesn't mean I don't know you. I see the way you pick up a brush and tenderly smooth the bristles, the way you look when you study a painting, the way your face seems to brighten when you walk through the door. What good are all these supplies if someone like you cannot use them?"

No one—*no one*—in her entire life had ever talked to her like that or had ever seen her that intimately before. Not even Tim. She was scared and excited at the same time.

And so they had worked out a deal. She'd come two mornings a week when the kids were in school to do the ordering and neaten the displays, and he would give her painting lessons and supplies. Her will had found its way.

Tim wasn't sure about the arrangement. "So how much does that work out an hour if he was paying you?"

"Oh, Tim, that's not the point."

"Seriously, getting a salary and then paying him may be a better arrangement."

"Trust me, it would not," she'd said, trying to be patient with his total lack of understanding about Daniel's generosity and her need to paint.

"I'm just saying," Tim went on.

"Look, he probably doesn't even really need help. He is just being kind so I can take his classes."

Tim looked suspicious. "Maybe I'd better go meet this guy first."

"No, it's nothing like that. Though thanks for thinking it. I think it's just that he can see how much I want to ... do this."

"You do?"

"Well, yeah, I think so."

"Look, we don't need charity. We can work something out if it's that important to you."

And so she had wrapped her arms around him and asked him to trust her. This was going to be perfect. And because he loved her, he had no choice.

Ruthie Barton. Who didn't know Ruthie? She was fortyish and wore clothes way too short and too tight, some even with leopard spots, and makeup that would have embarrassed her kids if she'd had custody of them. Ruthie was a free spirit who sailed through her life, leaving a trail of tragedy in her wake. Still, if you'd just met her, you'd never guess she was just surviving. She appeared to thrive off her failures. Say you just suffered a broken heart, and she'd beat your suffering by a mile. Say you were in love with a loser, and she'd name five she was still in love with. Say your parents had kicked you out of the house when you were a teen, and she'd tell you how she'd never had parents or a house.

So tasteless, tragic Ruthie and art? Hard to imagine for anyone except for Daniel. The first time Ruthie sashayed into his store—the night of the free food, actually—she had caught his attention. Not so much because he was afraid she would steal something, but that she was so raw with neediness.

"Nice place you have here," she'd said, wadding the soft cheesy thing into the side of her cheek so she could appear more gracious.

"Thank you," Daniel had replied.

"I remember when this place was just a hole-in-the-wall bookstore. Old bookstore, actually. I mean really, really old books. But, of course, I'd still come in. I like books." She felt he looked a little doubtful, so she continued, "I do. I liked looking at all those leathery books with tiny gold letters and their fancy words that didn't really make sense. Like, who really says *thou* and *thee?* Give me a break. But my favorites, what I especially liked, were his paperbacks with the buxomly smoldering women and the castles in the distance. I loved looking at the castles or old manor houses and just imagining. But"—she remembered now and leaned in toward him—"to be honest, there was one thing about this place that drove me crazy. The bookstore always smelled so musty. How'd you get the smell out of here anyway?"

"I guess the prior owner boxed it up with his books."

Ruthie rolled her eyes at her own stupidity. "Yeah, of course. Dah, it wasn't the place that was musty. It was those old books." She danced her fingers on the side of her leg as she searched for another interesting topic.

"So you like books," Daniel said. "Do you also like to paint?"

Ruthie cocked her head and considered the possibility, swallowing part of the cheese thing. "Never even thought about it, to tell the truth. But"—she shrugged—"I suppose I could do it. Heck, kindergarten kids paint."

"Indeed, they do," Daniel had said.

"Yes, indeed." Ruthie swallowed the rest of the cheese and pastry. "How much do you charge for lessons anyway?"

"Depends on what you want."

"Hey, I'd want the works. I won't say money is no object, though I wish I could, but still I can pay as good as anyone in this room."

"Why don't you stop by tomorrow and we can figure out what you want?"

Ruthie said sure, she'd be back, and then that old prune-faced teacher she'd always hated came right up and interrupted her conversation with the artist. Ruthie shot her a dirty look and went back to the food table where her best girlfriend, Lillian, was still sampling.

"I think he just hit on me," Ruthie said. There was definitely pride in her voice.

"Wow, really?"

"Yeah, he said for me to come back tomorrow so he can figure out what I want."

"Oh, now that sounds dangerous. He obviously didn't know who he was dealing with."

"Well, he's about to find out," Ruthie said, picking up a chopped-meat something and sniffing it. "Hope he is up to it," she said, and they both laughed. Ruthie sniffed the meat thing again and offered the appetizer to her friend.

"No, thanks," Lillian said, "I've had enough of those. They are pretty good, though. Really. Go ahead. It won't kill you. God knows you've eaten worse."

"Not when I was sober," Ruthie said. The two of them laughed at themselves again and then glanced back at the artist to see if he would notice them leaving. He didn't.

The next day Ruthie actually stopped back at the store. She'd almost forgotten about the painting thing herself, her being so distracted by the big fight she'd had with Max. Old up-yours Mad Max. Humph! Like he was the only creep in the world. Who needed him? He had bad teeth anyway. So she'd stomped out of his place with her purse and makeup case—she'd send Lillian back for the rest of her stuff—and made it all the way down Railroad Street before she stopped fuming enough to realize she didn't exactly know where she was headed. Damn Max driving her to such distraction that she had stormed off without thinking it through. So she had turned around and gone back.

"Forgit something?" he'd said sarcastically when she walked back in.

"Yeah, I forgot to kick your ass before I left."

Max laughed at her and nudged the leg of the chair opposite him at the table so it slid out for her. "Take a load off, and I'll get you some eggs."

Ruthie dropped her bags and headed for the bathroom. "Don't pepper them. You know I hate pepper."

Ruthie was in the middle of washing her hands, twenty seconds' worth of soaping, when she finally remembered the artist. Heck, she didn't have to go to work until three today. She could stop by, she supposed. The truth was, she was curious to see if he remembered her more than she was seriously interested in painting.

Daniel was with a customer, someone Ruthie didn't know— must be this lady didn't hang out in the same kind of places Ruthie did. Ruthie smirked at that. Always one to find the humor in every situation. Ruthie wandered around, touching things, picking them up, and putting them down. She eavesdropped on their conversation. Martian talk. Monet? Rembrandt? Ruthie pulled up her ever ready who-needs-you-anyway shield. What was she even doing here? I mean, really? Ruthie glanced back at the artist. He was definitely out of her league. The city type and good-looking. His teeth were perfect. She was a little suspicious about that, but she let it go. So he was good-looking and well-mannered, but the biggest obstacle, of course, was that she knew absolutely nothing about art. Sure, sure, she'd heard of artists like Monet and Rembrandt, but if someone had put three paintings together, she couldn't tell who painted what. Though Rembrandt sounded more like the nude-painting type than Monet. Monet? He sounded sissy. Maybe he painted flowers and butterflies. Hey, look at this, will ya? A book of Monet with water lilies, for crying out loud! Maybe she was a natural at figuring this art stuff out after all. Maybe this would really be something for her. A turn in her life. Ruth Mildred Barton, the famous artist from some little no-name place in Vermont, which suddenly became famous because of her art. Then let the la-di-das eat that for breakfast.

Daniel finished ringing up the lady's order, and she left. He came around to Ruthie because Ruthie had very coyly pretended to be so interested in this knife-looking thing that she hadn't noticed his customer had left.

"Glad to see you came back," he'd said.

Ruthie glanced up and asked him, just so he would know that she was interested in art too, what type of paintings Monet did. He told her Monet was most famous for his impressionist paintings.

"Oh, sure. Yeah," she stammered; she'd expected him to say *water lilies*. What was *impressionist,* for goodness' sake? "Well, anyway, I stopped by about the painting-class thing we talked about last night."

"I'm hoping to put together a small class. Five, maybe six, that meet once a week here at the shop."

Ruthie put the knife thing down. "Why me?"

He looked at her for a moment then told her that he'd been in this business long enough to have gained some instinct about people. "When I saw you last night, I knew that you would be just right for my class."

Ruthie wouldn't let him off that easy. She hadn't been born yesterday. "Like you haven't said that to every woman in town."

He shrugged. "Actually, I haven't. You were the only one last night whom I invited."

"Get out. Really?"

"Why does that surprise you?"

"Obvious reasons."

Daniel pretended—she could tell—not to understand.

"So are you willing to give it a try?" He asked.

"Trying is all I do," she'd said. "You could say I'm an expert at trying."

They had settled on a price; she'd tried to insist on paying more than he originally said. She wasn't a charity case no matter what he might think, but he had held firm to his fee. Then they had picked out some basic supplies she would need, and she was out of there and on her way to her waitress job at the Bar & Grill, asking herself what the hell she had signed up for. Just let Max make one stupid comment, and he'd be wondering what storm had blown through his sorry life.

Chapter 2

Daniel looked up as Pauline came through the store door. He glanced at the clock—four fifteen.

"Do you mind if I get a head start? I'll be quiet. I just couldn't wait to get here today."

"Not at all," Daniel said.

"It's just"—she said and giggled a little self-consciously as she slipped out of her worn denim jacket—"that I dreamed about my painting last night." She wanted to tell him how it had felt like love. How she could hardly breathe in her dream from wanting to be with it. But in her dream, when she had finally gotten to the shop—you know how crazy dreams can be, taking you places that don't make any sense, putting obstacles in your way that make you struggle to do the simplest things—anyway, when she had finally unveiled her painting ... it was all wrong. The colors had faded. The lines were more like spaghetti than art. She had stared in disbelief and then started to weep softly inside herself. But everyone else, Daniel and the other women in the class, had insisted it looked the same. She knew that it did not resemble in any way what she had intended. It was obvious that the essence of it had . . . left her. Why could no one but her see that? It had literally broken her heart. The depth, the vibrancy, and the beauty were gone. It was just flat color on canvas, and she didn't even want it anymore. And that truth, in itself, left her with an overwhelming emptiness. When she woke up, she could still feel that loss. It's crazy, she knew, but she just couldn't wait to get to the shop and see that her painting was just as she had left it.

"That's not unusual to dream about your painting," Daniel said. "When you are working on something, especially if there is a deadline, it is easy to carry that worry to bed."

Pauline unfolded her easel and tightened the leg screws. She wished she could tell Daniel; he would probably understand more than anyone, she supposed, but of course, she couldn't say any more because it was not just the dream. Lately, she had been getting forgetful, distracted in her duties by thinking about the painting and the show. It was selfish and dangerous. Jennifer had slipped in the bathtub because she had forgotten to put down the new fish stickies. She had scraped up the old ones and bleached the tub but had forgotten to put the new ones back in. And Jeffrey had gone to Cub Scouts without his belt because she couldn't find it. He was understandably hurt in his quiet little way. Jeffrey believed in being prepared, and she had let him down. And there were other things. Little things that probably didn't add up to anything, really, but still she knew her mistakes and was disappointed in herself.

"I will be glad when the show is over," she said. "It will be nice to go back to painting just for the joy of painting."

"It's not a contest, Pauline. It is just sharing what you do. What you see."

Pauline opened her paint case and suddenly felt a little better. There were her colors, her palette, and her turpentine cup. What was wrong with her? Daniel was right. It was just a showing of their paintings. All different. None right or wrong. Just six different women seeing things in their own way.

Daniel came out of the back with her canvas. He stood it up on her easel and stepped back. "Very nice," he said.

"I don't know. I've been thinking about where these shapes twist and go another direction. Well, it shouldn't be the same color. It should be more translucent or maybe like a softer light now shines on it from a different angle. Something. I don't know what to do."

"You're right. We can fix that. But let's start with your shading. See here where you have shadowed the curve of the circle onto the one behind it? This one. Here. What you need to do is shade the back one with the same angle of light as the front one."

Pauline nodded, now seeing it. Her shapes were not independent of one another. What light fell on one would also fall on the others around it. It was so obvious now.

"Hi, all," Ruthie said, bursting through the door. "It's our happy time again, and I brought brownies. Don't know what is wrong with me. Baking? What are the crazy planets up to?"

"Hope there isn't any illegal substances in them," Doris said, coming in right behind her.

Ruthie sat her plate of brownies on the counter. "Yeah right, just imagine the work we could put out then," she said. "It would all look like Pauline's."

Pauline flinched but didn't look over at them.

"Hey, come on. There isn't that much pot in the world to help you paint as good as Pauline," Doris said.

Ruthie grinned like a monkey and agreed. "Ain't that the truth? I may not understand her paintings, but they've got spunk."

Daniel relaxed and went into the back room to get the other canvases.

Doris got busy setting up her easel, and Ruthie wandered over to Pauline. "Hey, I didn't mean it like that."

"That's okay. I'm not sure I understand them either."

"I like this one. I really do," Ruthie said, nodding and staring at the colors. "You know what would look good? Some of that gold dust stuff. Just around the edges of the main globs to sort of highlight them. What do you think?"

"Maybe," Pauline said. "I'll think about it."

"Sure, okay. Well, help yourself to a brownie."

Pauline nodded, and Ruthie went to set up her easel. Pauline watched her. Ruthie had children. Two. Two girls. How does she live without them? How can she survive without being near them every day? Pauline knew that Ruthie had been married and somehow her ex-husband had gotten custody. How could that happen?

Carolyn came in next and set her easel up beside Doris. Doris smiled a welcome and began opening her paint tubes. Doris was a little relieved to see that Carolyn had gotten her hair cut since their last class. It actually had a little style. Still the same mousy brown, but at least it had more shape than the stringy shoulder-length mop she'd had. And Doris noticed, Carolyn had on a new, or new to the class, emerald-green blouse. It looked good on her. Might have even camouflaged a few pounds off.

Doris shook her head. That was so unkind. What was wrong with her lately? She had always prided herself on being generous to the less fortunate, but lately, she was thinking all kinds of mean things about everyone. She had always thought mean things about Frederick, but now, since that night, she felt angry at everyone. Of course, it was Frederick's fault. She was certain of that. She had never had a mean bone in her body until she'd chosen him.

Soft music came from the back room. Yanni or someone like him. Doris closed her eyes, breathed in, breathed out, and then slowly opened her eyes. There. Better. If she couldn't relax here, then where? She wouldn't give Frederick this part of her. She simply wouldn't. She wouldn't tell him about the show or display any of her paintings in their house. He didn't deserve it.

Doris looked at her painting. She was no artist and would be the first to admit it though she did give herself worlds of credit for stepping up and trying it. When she learned about the classes, she had instantly assured Daniel that she would participate. She had warned him that she was very much a novice and would, perhaps, be his neediest student. But now, she sighed, maybe she had bitten off more than she had imagined. How could she rescue this enough to actually present it to the town to critique?

"Daniel, when you have a moment . . ." Doris said when she saw him setting up the last canvas for Twilight. *Twilight?* Good grief, who would do that to a child? And especially one who exemplified, if anything, a cloud-shrouded midnight. What was with that girl? What boy did she think would want a toothpick with black fingernails and lipstick? And that hair. Sometimes it was black as coal, and sometimes she'd put some god-awful streak of unnatural burgundy running down one strand. Doris shook her head at the thought of Twilight though in all honesty, there was something about her that intrigued Doris. Maybe like some dead animal mangled on the roadside, stiff little legs sticking up, blood-smeared fur—the type of thing you didn't want to look at but you did. Doris didn't want to stare at Twilight and didn't want to encourage such self-destructive behavior by appearing interested, but she couldn't stop herself from watching her. Being the target of many jealous and narrow-minded women, Doris knew about all the different female types . . . except this one. Twilight was a mystery, and she suddenly wondered what Twilight was painting. Knives and skulls, she supposed.

Daniel appeared at her side, and Doris dismissed her thoughts of Twilight. "Look, just look at this . . . mud! Have you ever seen a mud-colored pear? I mean, it looks more like a potato. How artful is that?"

"Actually, there are brown pears. But if that is not what you intended, then I'm sure we can fix it."

"How?" Doris whined. "I've been working on it for two classes, and it just gets worse and worse."

"Let's practice on another canvas. I have some cheap ones, and you can draw several pears, then mix your colors and experiment until you find what you are looking for."

Doris nodded, not certain, and then an idea grabbed her. Of course, Daniel was talking about experimenting with paints, but suddenly, the idea of experimenting was just what she had been looking for. Oh, she wouldn't actually have to experiment, just let Frederick think she was. Yes. Suddenly, a weight had been lifted. She felt more like her old self. She just had needed a plan, and one was quickly coming to her.

"What is your light source?" Daniel asked.

"What? My what?"

"A window, the light from a lamp? Is the table your fruit is on inside a room or outside on a patio?"

Doris shrugged, a little annoyed now that he was getting into the painting when she had plans to devise.

"Your colors," he continued, "the shading, all depend on the light."

"Fine. Fine, then, it's from a window."

"Full sun, early evening light, filtered through branches?"

"Really, Daniel, how am I supposed to know?"

Daniel smiled at her, not a mocking smile, more just amused.

"I'll figure it out and get back with you," she'd finally said, and he had moved on to the next easel.

Doris tapped her acrylic nails on the lid of her paint box. While it was true that most of the men in town would be excited to have her choose them, she couldn't get involved in anything that could actually get messy. Just something that Frederick could think was messy. Forty years of the predictable, the comfortable, and the taking her for granted was about to end. Doris had probably giggled right out loud, for everyone paused to look at her.

"Isn't this fun?" Doris said and began mixing yellows and greens.

Eleanor sat at the kitchen table and listened to the phone ring. The answering machine came on, and she heard Trish's voice. "Mom. Mom, pick up. Mom?"

Eleanor flinched a little but did not move from her chair.

"Mom, you are never home anymore. Have you gotten a job? Are you sleeping? Where are you?"

There was a pause, and then the line went dead.

What was wrong with her? She had always hurried to the phone, hoping it was Trish, and now when it actually was, she didn't want to even pick it up. Eleanor looked down at her hands clasped on the table. Her hands were getting old. They were bony, and the veins were more pronounced. Bill had always liked her hands. Well, when they were dating anyway. He'd stroke the back of her hand with his thick thumb as gently as if her hand was made of satin. Bill had been a good husband, she supposed. Better than most she'd witnessed. He was a hard worker, fair and honest in all matters, and he was never one to let his temper fly. What would he think of her now? The question flamed her face.

Here Bill had only been gone a few months, and already she was going to bed alone and waking up alone, and.. . she wasn't suffering. She should be grieving. She should still be waiting for him to come home from work. She should be deeply saddened when she saw the empty spaces where his toothbrush and garden boots and reading glasses used to be. Of course, she hadn't had the heart to cook any of his favorite dishes or sell his old truck or sit in his TV chair, but still she wasn't behaving as a proper widow. Maybe she was in denial. Maybe she was acting, one could imagine, like someone who subconsciously expected their dearly departed to return one day. Like this time was a time to get through, to be someone else, and to live like she was someone else, and then she could one day go back to her real life. Except if no one was listening or judging, she would have to admit that she did not want to go back to her real life. She wanted to keep pretending that she actually was that someone else who could be seen.

Clearly, she knew she was being foolish about Daniel. When Eleanor wasn't near him, she could see that he was just a pleasant man who had that special charm that made everyone want to be around him. He had that gift of making everyone feel worthy. She saw it with the other women in the painting class. He made them feel worthy of their dreams, and they all, in a way, loved Daniel for that rare gift.

"But what is my dream?" Eleanor whispered to the empty room. What was she looking for around that turn in the road?

The phone suddenly rang out in the quiet, and Eleanor startled then picked it up. "Hello."

"Mom, for God's sake, where have you been? I've been calling and calling."

"Oh. I'm sorry, dear. What is it you need?"

"Need? I'm calling because I'm concerned. What's going on with you?"

"What do you mean? I'm fine."

"Well, your snoopy-ass neighbor doesn't think you are fine. She calls with all this crap about you not doing well and dying of a broken heart and going out to Dad's grave every day and suffering."

"I don't do that. I'm fine. Really."

There was a pause, then Trish said, "You don't sound fine."

"1 am."

"Okay, then. So we'll leave it at that, but you have to tell your snoopy-ass neighbor to stop calling me if she doesn't know what the hell she is talking about. Because if you don't tell her and she calls me again . . ."

"I'll take care of it. Thanks for checking on me."

"Yeah. Okay. I've gotta go."

"Good-bye, dear," Eleanor said and gently returned the phone to its base. "Oh, Fran," Eleanor said with a shake of her head, "you old snoopy ass."

Milly was drying the dinner dishes, careful to wipe the water off gently so as not to be accused of trying to wear the design off Fran's everyday china, when something caught her eye. She leaned over the counter and squinted out the window. Why, there was Eleanor coming across the street with a dish in her hands. Looked like she was coming straight for their house.

"Fran, Eleanor is coming," Milly said, hurrying into the living room, where Fran was watching *Wheel of Fortune.*

"What?" Fran said, scowling up at her sister.

"It's Eleanor from across the street, she is coming here."

Fran pushed herself up from her chair. "I know where Eleanor lives for pity's sake. Now get back in the kitchen with that dripping plate." Fran looked through the kitchen doorway and out the window just to be certain Milly was right, then she lowered the sound on the TV and went to the door.

Eleanor smiled when Fran opened the door before she even knocked. "Good evening."

Fran nodded. "What brings you visiting?"

Eleanor extended the pie dish. "I just felt like cooking again and didn't want to eat this cherry pie all by myself, so I was hoping you and Milly could take some of it off my hands."

Fran could feel Milly sneaking up behind her. "That would not be a problem for us. I remember Bill was quite proud of your cherry pies."

"He was," Eleanor said, still holding out the pie.

Fran took the pie and invited Eleanor in, nearly stepping on Milly as she moved away from the door so Eleanor could come inside. "Good grief, Milly, you trying to get a body killed? Here, take this into the kitchen."

"Actually," Eleanor said, "I can't stay long. I'm expecting a call from Trish, but I did want you to know that I won't be going to the cemetery every day any longer. I think I have worked through the hard part. Guess we all have our own way of handling things."

"Good," Fran said, nodding. "That's good. Besides, Bill isn't there anyway."

Milly gasped, the pie trembling in her hands.

"Once the soul leaves the body, then don't matter where the body is, that person isn't there. That's why I'm going to be cremated. No sense in rotting and shriveling away to dust when I can just get it over with right away."

Milly ran to the kitchen.

"That's, ah, that's very sensible," Eleanor said.

"Wish I'd thought of it when Philip died. It would have saved me a ton of money too."

"Yes, well, I had better get home. Don't want to miss Trish's call. She worries if I am not there to answer the phone."

"Sure. Sure," Fran said. "And thanks for the pie."

Eleanor nodded and turned to leave.

Milly stood weak-kneed at the sink and watched as poor, poor Eleanor crossed the street and went up her front steps. Milly looked down at the cherry pie, and tears gathered in her eyes. This beautiful pie. Crust flaky and golden. Cherries juicy, red, and sweet. One perfect piece cut out. It was suddenly the saddest thing Milly might have ever seen. Bill's favorite pie. Baked in loving memory of him and then delivered to the most unappreciative and cruel . . . yes, cruel. What Fran had said was bone-deep cruel and unforgivable. Rotting and shriveling into dust! How could Fran say such a thing to poor Eleanor?

Milly glanced up to see the front door close behind Eleanor, and a wet tear broke loose and streaked down her cheek.

"You going to stand there all day hovering over that pie, or are you going to wake up and cut me a piece?"

Milly wiped the wet from her face with the palm of her hand and pulled a clean knife out of the dish drainer. "Would you like ice cream with your pie?" she asked, forgetting for the first time in five years to feel appreciative of Fran's generosity of sharing her home with her inadequate, bumbling sister.

⸻⟋∾∾⟋∾∾⟋⸻

Frederick walked into the kitchen and frowned. "Where's dinner? Are we going out tonight?"

Doris finished the glass of Cabernet and rinsed out the glass before putting it in the dishwasher. She felt Frederick waiting for an answer. She was nearly giddy inside. Doris then turned back to him and smiled ever so mysteriously, her amazing dimples barely dimpling. "We are not going out. I am. I have a . . . well, something to do at the art store."

"You spend a lot of time at that place."

Doris flourished past him. "Yes. Yes, I do. Please don't wait up for me. Things are getting intense there, and I don't know when I will be home."

"Intense? What the hell does that mean?"

She paused by the hall table to pick up her purse. She looked at him and shook her head. "I doubt you would really understand. It's just, you know, art stuff."

She glanced at the long windows beside the front door before she backed out of the driveway. She had hoped to see Frederick's worried face watching her leave. Well, never mind, he was worrying. She was certain of it.

Doris arrived at the store just as Daniel was turning the Open sign to Closed. She parked right in front, in case Frederick drove past the store, and waited for Daniel to lock up and meet her on the sidewalk.

"The entrance is on the side street here at the corner," Doris said, walking close beside Daniel in case Frederick was watching with binoculars from somewhere. "But I am certain it will be perfect. We can put a big banner hanging between these two buildings so everyone can find us. Like it would be hard in this town." She laughed at herself. "Still, it would be nice. Of course, I will get the banner professionally made so we look real."

Daniel smiled. "We are real."

"Oh, you know what I mean. We are all beginners, and well, some of us—I won't mention names so I won't have to mention myself—are not, to be honest, very good."

"The art show will answer that. I'm certain all of you will be pleasantly surprised."

"*Surprised* would be the right word. And though I'll throw my work out there anyway, I have to tell you that this is the first thing in my life I have felt did not, in any way, represent my true talents. I'm trying, but painting doesn't feel natural to me. Maybe," she said, pausing before the door with the key in her hand, "maybe it's just too confining for my talents. I'm used to putting on big events. Decorating for grand occasions. Pulling colors of fabric and flowers and food together. No one can top me in that department."

"I'm certain they can't," Daniel said, following her into the Rotary Hall.

Doris turned on the light and Daniel looked around. "You will never recognize this place when I get through with it," Doris said. "I have plans. It will be amazing. A real event."

"I see," Daniel said. "A real event for not real artists."

Doris laughed loudly in case Frederick was listening outside the door. "If we can't bewilder and impress them with our art, we will dazzle them with our presentation."

"I can hardly wait," Daniel said.

"So let's get comfortable and talk details, and then you can take me to dinner," Doris said.

"You are a hard woman to say no to," Daniel said and followed her to the receptionist desk to draw up their staging and traffic flow.

⸺⁓⦾⧜⦾⁓⸺

Ruthie finished the paperback and closed it. The cover was so promising. A beautiful and ever so innocent-looking maiden with thick red hair and startling green eyes, holding a basket of freshly picked wildflowers. Behind her was her handsome hero on a muscular white steed. And behind him, a huge manor house. All the ingredients for a beautiful tale. But it was flat. Predictable. You could skim over most of it because it was so trite. "Please, God, don't let me outgrow fantasy. I have nothing to replace it."

Ruthie put the book on the nightstand and turned out the light. Max had been asleep for an hour or so. His occasional snoring and restless leg syndrome were distractions, but she couldn't blame him for her dissatisfaction of the book or her life. It was the painting that was to blame. She never should have started it. Every Tuesday she would pick up her brush and dab on images of her dreams. They were just hints of people and places. Nothing with detail, but one would know it was a woman in a full gown or a weeping willow tree or the ghost of a horse. She would dab away and then stand back to see if it was right. But how could it be right if nothing was clear? If it was only the hint of itself?

Ruthie got up and left the bedroom. She settled in a chair by the window and stared out at the circle of streetlight on the sidewalk in front of their shabby apartment. It was so sad. That lone circle of light. She had never noticed how sad it was before, it was probably the painting's fault. Now she was actually looking at things. And most of the things made her sad. She missed her girls. She missed her brief married life when she was actually pretending to be happy and normal. But that didn't work. Ruthie eventually surfaced, and it was best to leave. To take herself out of all their lives. She had hoped, so selfishly, that they would remember the good times when she was pretending and forget the bad times when she wasn't.

Her whole life, until her brief time with Robert, had been a scam. It's how she got through when she had nothing else to give. Make people laugh at you, and they stop judging. Make them feel superior to you, and suddenly, you are not a threat. Pretend they are smarter than you, and they will help you and give you second chances. Everyone, she had discovered, liked to feel good about themselves, and helping a lesser soul always worked for them and for her. This scam of a person had been at it so long Ruthie worried she didn't know if there was a real her inside or just this sad, pathetic clown. And now, because of the painting, she wasn't feeling as funny, as free to be outrageous, or as proficient at hiding her feelings as she had thought. She couldn't lose herself in romantic daydreams or fantasies of anything changing in her life. Who she was and where she was at this moment were all she would ever have. Damn that painting!

Tuesday arrived again, and all were busy in front of their easels. Eleanor was concentrating on getting the light on the beginning of the path through the forest lighter than its turn into the forest. She wanted to paint it almost sun-drenched because she had just realized that one could envision oneself walking out of the forest as well as walking into it. And if someone stood in front of her painting and smiled softly at it, then she would know that was exactly what they were thinking. It could be a hopeful journey forward as well as a somber leaving of a place. Her first painting had been an autumn scene, but this one she painted for spring. Fresh tender greens. Yellow dandelions dotted through the new grass. She somehow, though she couldn't define it or understand it, felt a little optimistic that this would be her best painting.

Doris had an array of canvases propped up around her. She mixed and stirred her colors. She squinted and scanned from one to the other. She liked the pear color on this test canvas but forgot which paint blob she had used. "Daniel, can you come and help me here?" She knew, of course, that her painting skills were no better than a color-blind twelve-year-old, but it didn't matter. Tonight she had left the house dressed in a stunning and, she would immodestly admit, figure-enhancing sapphire blouse. She wore tight jeans, and her hair had just been professionally styled and dyed a golden blond. Yes, in the right light it was pure gold. She had gone into Frederick's den to remind him that it was Tuesday and she was on her way to the art studio. She even went over to the chair where he was sitting to lean in, her cleavage ever so close to his face, and kiss him on his forehead, the fragrance of her new perfume bewildering him, she was certain. So if he had left the comfort of his chair and was, at this moment, standing across the street hidden in the evening shadows, she knew he could see Daniel coming to stand next to her, advising her, and of course, she would smile and tilt her head so coyly, and perhaps, she would even, in some intimate gesture, just reach out and touch Daniel's arm.

Pauline stood with one crimson-tipped brush clenched between her teeth and was dabbing at a glob of dark blue, so dark it was almost night, then she, with the steadiest of hand, painted the inside curl of the crimson ribbon. It wasn't exactly a ribbon, of course, because nothing she painted was a thing but rather a shape. A circle, a spiral, a long rectangle that, at the end, folded back in the opposite direction. She loved this stuff even though she didn't understand it. And that worried her a lot. How was she going to explain it to the confused townspeople when they saw it at the art show? No one she knew had such things as this in their homes. Would they wander home, gossiping about what was wrong with Pauline? Would they look at her children to see if this strangeness was hereditary? How could something that made her heart glad cause her such turmoil?

Ruthie glanced at Pauline's painting and wondered how Pauline could put so much detail into nothing when she herself couldn't get detail into something. She had tried a smaller brush with a fine point, but she couldn't make it work. There were no sharp outlines in Ruthie's paintings, not even her castles. If she was not talented enough to paint a human face, she should, at least, be able to paint a straight wall. If she stood close to her painting, even she could barely guess what it was. She dabbed muted colors into some sort of form, and when she stepped back, it somewhat looked like the thing she was trying to paint. Daniel seemed to get it. He encouraged her to relax and let it be what it was. Sure, relax. Ruthie was good at letting things be what they were. She was her best when there were no expectations or rules.

Caroline pushed up the sleeves of her worn gray sweater. The sweater might have even been her husband's by the way it fit her. It was clean but formless. Her listless brown hair was tucked behind her ears, and her glasses were perched halfway down her nose. Her skin was flawless, lacking the fine stress lines one might expect from someone living with a drunk. Oh, she knew what the town thought of Charlie. He was a drunk. He was a sad case. But she loved him for the deep sensitivities that forced him to soften his sadness and fears with drink. Charlie worked at the retirement home just outside town. He would come home every day and share the suffering and loss he had witnessed. "Sadie passed last night. I had to box up her personal things. She had a collection of cards from her only son that she hadn't seen in thirty years. Really, thirty years and he could never come and visit his mother. Imagine the sadness these cards brought her." Or "Ralph lost his foot to diabetes. He'll just give up now, I know it. I could see when he was worrying about his surgery that he'd made up his mind to just sit and wait for death." How could any of these women understand Charlie's goodness? His disappointments? How could they understand his sadness that she would never be able to have his children? No. No, she could never leave or change such a wonderful man. Caroline dabbed her thin, finely-pointed brush into the brown paint and meticulously worked on the wood grain of the rocking chair on the white front porch.

Twilight was not exactly Twilight tonight. Perhaps no one else noticed in their rush to finish their paintings for the showing in a week and a half, but there were things that were slightly different about her. Of course, she hadn't come in wearing some silly pink girl clothes or white tennis shoes or a crucifix, but if they had really looked, they would have seen someone wearing their black on the outside but not as certain she felt that way inside any longer. It felt weird, actually, to be conscious of herself. She had hidden inside her darkness so long she had just accepted it. She had a few acquaintances who were like her, but mostly, she was a loner. She read science fiction and drew gothic figures that were quite detailed, thinking that one day she might be a designer for that sort of look. Or maybe she'd just work in a store that sold her kind of stuff. Whenever she got the courage to leave home for the city, of course.

She'd have to admit that she had been as surprised as anyone when she had stepped into this shop and felt the draw to paint with these colors. She'd picked up the tubes of color one at a time and held them in her hand. Yellow. Red. Blue. And white. White was pretty when you looked right at it. When it was only itself and not around or behind anything else. Just white. Her pictures were still darker in tone and subject than the other women's paintings. Anyone would be able to sort out hers from the rest. But even though her figures were gaunt and dark eyed, she actually needed the colors to make them real. Black wasn't just black, Daniel had said. Black needed color to bring it to life.

Tonight Twilight was reworking the first painting she had ever done. It was a dark room, the one window shrouded in heavy drapes, lots of bookshelves, a round table draped in a floor-length cloth. On the table were a candlestick, an open book lying faceup, and a framed drawing of a tree—a weeping willow tree that touched the ground. That was all. A solitary tree in a black frame. There was a straight- backed chair beside the table with a woman sitting, rigid, somber, and staring straight out of the painting right at you. Twilight liked this woman, but she could see how the figure might leave some a little uneasy.

Twilight twisted off the cap of the white paint. She squeezed out a small dab. She painted a white flame on the candle. No yellow or orange. Pure white. She added tiny touches of white about the room. On the right side of the chairback. The right side of the picture frame. On the right side of the open bookbinding. On the right side of the table drape. Then in the top right corner of the room, she painted the white shape of an ... angel. No detail. But anyone would know what it was. She then stepped back and looked at the difference it had made. It changed everything—everything in the room whether Twilight had accented it with white or not. Twilight's eyes misted a little at the sight.

"What?" Carolyn asked, thinking Twilight was upset over a mistake she had made. "What's wrong?"

Twilight glanced over at Carolyn.

"Do you believe in God?"

"What?" Carolyn shook her head as though she hadn't understood.

"Do you believe in God?"

Now everyone in the room had stopped painting and was frozen in place. Where did that question come from? That was not a question anyone in class expected and, certainly, not one they would expect from Twilight.

Carolyn flushed and glanced around for help from someone else. They all stood waiting.

"Do any of you believe in God?"

"Well, of course, we do," Doris finally blurted out. "We aren't heathens. We go to church."

"But do you really believe that God is real? That he created all this? That he is actually somewhere right now? Not just in church, but everywhere?"

"Where is this coming from? I mean, really, why are you talking like this in art class?" Doris was frowning now.

Twilight looked down at the brush in her hands. "A ... a little girl asked me yesterday if I was for the devil."

"Good gracious," Eleanor whispered. Everyone else waited, not certain what was happening.

Twilight lifted her head and looked back at her painting. "I told her no. Then she asked me that if I was for God, then why did I dress like this? I told her it was just what I liked to wear. She asked me why when there were so many pretty things? I told her I didn't feel pretty. And she said that if I believed in God, then I had to believe I was pretty because God only made pretty things."

"Well, I can tell you that isn't exactly true. I've seen some pretty ugly sights in my day," Ruthie said, trying to lighten the conversation. "Might even have been one of those ugly sights myself once or twice."

"Oh, now don't go feeling bad about what little kids say," Pauline said, walking away from her easel to give Twilight a motherly hug. "They repeat things they hear and . . ." Pauline stopped and stared at Twilight's canvas. "An angel? Is that an angel?"

Twilight nodded.

Angel? The other women came to see. No one spoke, just gathered together with their paintbrushes still in their hands and stared at the canvas.

Daniel hadn't moved. "I believe God is everywhere," he said. "And I believe in angels."

What? The women all pulled back. What was going on here?

"Of course, he does. We all do. What's the big surprise? Let's just get back to work," Doris said and moved away from that dark child's disturbing painting to the success of her golden pear.

Slowly the others returned to their easels, but the mood had been broken. It was difficult to pick up the creative flow they had before Twilight's intrusion.

"I want to believe he is real," Carolyn finally said.

"Good grief," Doris exploded. "Is this a painting class or a church meeting?"

"Sorry," Twilight murmured. "I just didn't know who else to ask."

"No apology necessary," Daniel said, going to Twilight's side and looking for the first time at her painting. "Wow," he said softly. "Perfect. Except, I'm curious, did you leave the white off the woman because she was the lone thing in the room who was not aware of the angel or touched by the light? Or are you just not finished yet?"

"I don't know," Twilight said. "I thought about it, I wanted to add it, but I couldn't add the light and not change her. Wouldn't she have to be changed if the light touched her?"

"Most definitely," Daniel said and smiled. "If you'd like, you can stay after class, and we can discuss that further."

"I'd like to stay," Carolyn said. "If it is okay."

"Me too," Eleanor said.

Ruthie said she had no reason to hurry home. Pauline said she'd love to stay, but the kids always waited for her to tuck them in. Doris, of course, even though she was annoyed with this whole matter, could not be left out. Besides, the later she got home, the more time Frederick would have to wait and think.

"Thanks," Twilight said.

"Now," Daniel said, "does anyone else have any questions or need help before we clean up?"

The easels were taken down, the canvases moved safely into the back room, and paint boxes tidied and secured. The shop looked like itself again. But it didn't feel like itself again. There was a quiet sort of worry and uncertainty in the air. What would Daniel have to say about Twilight's painting? Or God? Was he going to talk about God or the light from the angel? None of them knew what they expected or wanted to hear; they just knew that they didn't want to miss whatever it was. Shared insight into anything was rare in their worlds.

"I wish there was room for us to get comfortable, but I'm afraid I don't have the luxury of a seating area," Daniel said. "If you don't mind sitting on crates, we can go into the back."

Everyone glanced around at one another. Sure. Sure, why not?

Pauline had gone home, so the five of them followed Daniel through the curtain behind the cash register. Each found a box or crate and sat down facing Daniel. It felt like grade school or maybe a covert meeting place where national secrets were shared. Carolyn half wished now that she had just gone home, and Doris was wondering if Frederick would wait outside however long this took. It was a warm night. The mosquitoes might have chased him off. Eleanor sat straight-backed, hands in her lap as Twilight picked at her black fingernail polish.

"Well," Ruthie blurted, her loudness startling the others, "you have our undivided attention. Bring it!"

Daniel took Twilight's painting and propped it up on a box where everyone could see. He studied it a moment, sadness frowning his face, and then he turned and looked into each of their waiting faces. "I've never told anyone about this, but Twilight's painting is a clear sign that it's time to share what I know. Not just what I believe, but what I know."

Everyone glanced back at the painting. Even Doris, though she didn't care for that type of art, was so intrigued she forgot to think about Frederick.

"Growing up I was, I assume, like most of you. I went to church with my family. I got through it and then went back to my life. When I got my license and a job, I stopped going. It wasn't until I met my wife that I went back. I went back for her, not for myself, so I still got nothing out of going, really. But Jill got it. She would be radiant when we walked out after the service. She always had to stop and shake the minister's hand and tell him how brilliant his sermons were. And she was sincere. So when she got terminal cancer, I had to wonder about her God. It didn't make any sense. Her continued faith actually irritated me. I was angry at the cancer, at God, and maybe some at her for her unwavering trust in God's love. It all seemed so pointless if God was not going to save her. We knew that she was dying. And God was not even letting her die in a gentle and painless way."

Daniel paused, and everyone waited. This might be too sad to endure. They didn't understand yet what his heartbreaking story could possibly have to do with Twilight's dark and confusing painting.

"But," Daniel went on, "Jill was right, and she left me and all of you the most amazing miracle. I was with her at the end. She was so weak she had stopped talking. Her thin hand was too limp to hold tight to mine. But in her last moments, she opened her eyes and looked into the corner of the room. She smiled and asked me if I could see the angels there. They had come for her, and she was ready. She told them yes, yes, she was ready, and she closed her eyes and smiled contentedly as she breathed her last breath."

"For real?" Twilight asked. "She saw angels?"

"I believe that she did, yes. I have never told anyone else about this, but your painting, with the angel in the corner, told me it was time to share Jill's story."

The women glanced around at one another. It would be great to believe in angels. And they had probably all thought they did, but thinking you believed and knowing you believed were two different levels.

"After Jill's funeral, I went to the bookstore and bought all the books I could find on near-death experiences and books written by people who were with the dying at the end. I had to believe that Jill was somewhere. I wanted to believe what she saw. That when she left me, she was not afraid, but truly happy."

"So what did the books say?" Doris asked.

"Pretty much what I experienced with Jill."

"Well," Ruthie said, "why haven't you told everyone? Why haven't you written a book?"

Daniel shrugged and shook his head. "I believe Jill saw angels. I believe they took her to heaven. I believe God welcomed her home. I just, I guess, didn't want to do anything that finalized that belief. I didn't want to actually let her go, and writing about it, talking about it, would make it real in the world, not just in my head." He turned his back to them and stared at the painting. "What do you think, Twilight, will the light touch her or not?"

"Yes," Twilight whispered. "I will change her."

Tears stung Carolyn's eyes, and she rubbed them away. She suddenly needed to get home to Charlie.

Ruthie shifted uncomfortably on her crate. This was all too much to wrap your mind around. It would be nice to think angels came and escorted you to heaven, but on the other hand, who wanted to believe that God was always watching?

Eleanor stood up and smoothed the wrinkles from the front of her painting smock. She hadn't actually thought about Bill in heaven. He wasn't a religious man—never set foot in a church unless it was a wedding or funeral. But he was a good man. Surely, God would welcome him. She suddenly wished she had been there the moment he died instead of finding him on the floor when it was too late to help him or know if he had seen his own angel.

"I'm sorry about your wife," Doris said. "But I think you should share her story. I mean how many miracles do we get to see or hear about? Maybe you could come to my church and talk to the minister. He could help you present it to the congregation. I can, maybe, set up a tasteful reception after the service so people could meet you and you could answer questions." Really, how grand would it be to present such an amazing story to these simple town folks? Here she was, taking painting lessons from someone whose wife actually saw angels.

"Thanks, Doris, but I think I'll just keep it to this group for now. I had just intended to answer Twilight's question about believing in God, but her painting suddenly felt like a clear sign to share more."

"Thank you," Twilight said, "tonight has changed everything."

"I hope so," Daniel said, "I hope so." He stepped to the curtain and pulled it aside so they could leave through the shop door. One by one they passed in front of him. Carolyn smiled sadly at him. Ruthie looked a little worried. Eleanor paused and thanked him. Doris said to just let her know when he was ready to go public. And Twilight asked him if he still had any of those books he had talked about. He told her he did and would be happy to bring some to the shop if she wanted to come by and get them.

He followed them to the door and watched them depart in their different directions. He looked up at the clear, starry night. "Sure, you're there singing and dancing and sitting at the feet of Jesus," he said, smiling. "And here I have just stepped into the unknown with all these women. When you get a minute," he said to Jill, "ask God for a little guidance for me. I'm afraid I'm going to need it."

Chapter 3

"Humph," Fran said, putting her ice cream bowl in the sink. "She's getting home later than last week."

Milly clicked her knitting needles as she flew through the yarn of her next afghan. This one was blue and green. Fran told her it was hideous. Who would have a room that would go with both blue and green, especially those strong shades of blue and green that fought each other for dominance? "I like it," Milly had said.

Fran came back into the living room and dropped down into her chair with an "Oomph!"

"Maybe you'd better skip the ice cream at night," Milly mumbled.

"What? Did you say something?"

"Nothing that matters," Milly said, watching the rerun of her favorite *Waltons* show as her needles clicked on.

"You've seen this one a million times," Fran grumbled. "Don't forget *The Real Housewives of New Jersey* comes on in six minutes."

"Oh, I won't forget," Milly said sweetly. "I have to go into my room and call Harry anyway. He and Margie invited me over for a few days. I think I'll go this time."

Fran perked up straight in her chair. "Well, well, what brought this about? He trying to wheedle you out of his inheritance before you're even dead?"

Milly smiled at Fran, knowing Fran expected her to be flustered and defend her son and knowing that throwing out the idea of Milly's own death was cruel. But Milly took a breath and pretended she hadn't heard it. "Perhaps he will. But anyway, I have some business to take care of while I am there."

"Like what?"

"Oh, just business. I think all my grandchildren will be home this weekend also. It's Margie's birthday on Saturday, you know."

"Humph, you've never been invited for her birthday before."

Milly stopped knitting. "Now how do you know that? Maybe I have and just haven't chosen to go."

Fran snorted a laugh. "Right."

"Yes, anyway," Milly went on as she gathered her knitting yarn and her blue-green afghan and laid it in her knitting basket, "I think I will go make that call."

Fran sank back in her chair. "I can drive you if you aren't up to it," she offered.

"Oh, it's only fifty miles. I can easily do it. I think I'll go tomorrow."

Fran watched her sister go into her room and close the door. It wasn't that Fran considered herself especially suspicious, but she had a feeling that Milly was up to something. She just hadn't been herself lately, mumbling stuff under her breath, crossing herself like she was some religious zealot. Well, just let her go to her son's house. They would be plenty grateful to be rid of her when they sent her back. Milly was a fidgeter, always needing to be doing something. Not everyone would have the patience to put up with that, especially if they hadn't grown up sharing a room with someone like that. It was nerve-racking just sitting in a room with her constant polishing or picking lint or endlessly clicking her knitting needles to make hideous things that no one would even want to accept for free. Now she had some harebrained idea that she'd visit her son and they wouldn't be anxious to see her leave. Ms. La-di-da and her son and grandchildren. Humph! Oh good, finally, there were those naughty, rude housewives. Fran had her favorites and, of course, the ones she could barely stand to look at when they came into a room.

Doris thought about Daniel's story as she drove home. Of course, he had to believe his wife. Of course, his wife wanted to see angels. But still, Doris wasn't convinced. Especially when he said he didn't want other people to know. She would ask her minister to meet with her after church on Sunday and see what he thought. Shouldn't Daniel tell everyone if it were true? She would certainly want to share that experience if she'd been witness to it. It was, admittedly, somewhat creepy that Twilight randomly stuck that angel-looking thing in the corner of her painting. Twilight—now there was a strange child, dressing like the daughter of doom and then being so disturbed when someone asked her if she leaned to the dark side. Hadn't Doris always lived by the standard of "what you see is what you get"? Lord knows,

Doris wouldn't have landed the life she had if she hadn't presented her best at all times or if she had let herself go or dressed like death. It was so bizarre. Twilight, of all people.

Doris pulled up in front of her house. The porch light was on. There were two other cars in her driveway. Cars, she recognized, as belonging to some of Frederick's old cronies. She got out of her car and paused when she passed the cars to test them with her hand and see if the hoods were still warm. Frederick might have hurried home from watching her and then just invited his friends over to make it appear that he'd been home all the time. The hoods were the temperature of the night air. They had been there awhile. Still, she conceded, she had stayed later than usual, so he might have planned for her usual time at painting class.

Doris could hear their voices when she entered the foyer. They were in Frederick's den, playing poker. She was tempted to walk past unnoticed and just go upstairs, but then she remembered how fabulous she looked tonight. She had better stop by the card table and remind Frederick whom he was married to and let his potbellied, bald old friends compare her to their wives.

"Ahh, you're home," Frederick said when she entered the room. "How did my little Rembrandt do tonight?"

Chet and Ed laughed, and she ignored them. "Oh," she said, "Daniel was especially brilliant tonight. Sorry to be getting home so late, but well. . ." She just left it at that.

The men pretended not to get her inference and went back to their game. Doris walked past the table, in case her perfume had any lingering scent, then picked up an empty chip bowl coated with grease residue and a plate that was littered with gnawed chicken-wing bones. Maybe Frederick had actually been here enjoying himself all evening.

Doris left the room and sat the stinky dishes on the kitchen counter, not even sliding the chicken bones into the trash, and went up to her room. She went in and closed the door then leaned back against it in the dark. Daniel was suffering for a wife he didn't have, and Frederick was such a coldhearted idiot he didn't even see or smell the wife he did have. Frederick was ruining her life. That's all there was to it. She had to give up. She had to accept her fate and make a new plan—a plan where Frederick couldn't disappoint her, where she would refuse to see him and make a good life for herself before that angel came for her.

Doris went to Frederick's closet and took down his travel toiletry bag and then filled it with what he would need for tonight and the next morning. She got his pajama bottoms and folded them. She went back into his closet and picked out work clothes and clean underwear for him. She opened the bedroom door and piled them neatly on the floor in front of her door. Then she closed the door and locked it. She had never, never locked Frederick from their room before. Not once in all their long marriage. But she knew she was not up to any surprise shoulder kisses tonight. Her heart was irretrievably broken. God only knew what she would do to him if he ever tried any of that crap on her again.

Eleanor lay in her bed, legs straight and hands clasped on her abdomen, and was staring through the darkness at the tiny green light of the smoke detector on her ceiling. So much to think about. Hearing Daniel's story made her want to believe in God. In angels. And she would have easily said that she did . . . until tonight. This was so much more than saying it. She had witnessed real belief tonight. She'd heard the wonder in Daniel's voice when he told them Jill had left them all a miracle. *A miracle.* Eleanor never thought of one leaving a miracle for others when they died. But if you believed Daniel, and she did, then she had to believe actual angels were in that hospital room, waiting for Jill to go with them.

Eleanor had never read the Bible. She didn't know anyone who had, actually. She had tried once, and it had overwhelmed her. The deeper she went, the more frightened she had become of God's wrath. She gave up. She wondered if she would understand it better now that she believed it all to be true. Oh, of course, she had never questioned the truth of the Bible, but now it would be real. Like she knew people who were actually with God. She now believed he sent his angels to help people. How many times had she halfheartedly told Trish that she must have a guardian angel watching over her? What if Trish actually did? What if Eleanor herself actually had one? This whole other realm was somewhat frightening.

Eleanor turned and stretched to reach the bedside lamp. She clicked it on and lay back. She took a deep, slow breath and calmed her heart. She wished Bill was beside her. Oh, she wouldn't be able to discuss this with him. He wouldn't have believed it. He might even have been as threatened by it as he had been of her painting or anything else she ever did outside of their tiny world. No, they wouldn't explore these new thoughts together, but it would have been a comfort just to feel him there beside her while she worked it out.

Tomorrow, she promised herself, she would get out the family Bible and try to read it again. Maybe she'd even go to church on Sunday. Just to see what they were saying there. To see if the parishioners seemed to be getting the message or if they were just sitting dutifully there like Daniel said he used to do. Before Jill. Eleanor wondered about Jill. Daniel had described her as radiant. Eleanor knew, she herself had never been radiant. Not to herself or anyone else. How did it feel to be radiant? How did it feel to know someone else thought you were? Eleanor envied the confidence and peace Jill must have had when Jill believed she was loved by Daniel and God.

The sleeping pill Eleanor had taken began to relax her. She hadn't taken a sleeping pill since Trish had moved to Florida. Eleanor closed her eyes and turned her face away from the lamp.

———⚬⚬⚬⚬⚬———

Twilight came out of her room dressed in a white blouse with black slacks and a black sweater. Her hair was pulled back from her face and tied at the nape of her neck with a white ribbon. She carried her black backpack. She wore no lipstick, and the black polish had been removed from her fingernails. The white blouse was one she had found in the farthest back corner of her closet. Her mother insisted she have something normal to wear if she visited her grandmother.

Her parents saw this change and glanced at each other and then back at her. They were never certain what to expect from Elizabeth. She had always been a different sort of child. They knew that she even referred to herself as Twilight outside the family. Fortunately, she had not gotten into the tattoos and piercings that they had seen on other strange children. The blackness and silence were unnerving enough.

"I'm going to stay with Gram for a while. Maybe just tonight. I don't know," Elizabeth said.

"Okay. Does she know you are coming?" her mother asked.

"Yes. I called her, and she said it was okay."

Elizabeth's father stood up and fished his car keys out of his pocket. "You want to ride along, Sue?"

Elizabeth's mother shook her head. "I'll get the kitchen cleaned while you are gone. But give your mom my love."

Elizabeth followed her father out to the car. They were down to the end of her street before he asked her if she was all right.

"I think I will be."

"Good," he said, and they rode the rest of the way in silence. Her father didn't go in with her. He had never understood what went on with Elizabeth, and even if he did, he was confident that he wasn't the problem or the answer.

Elizabeth walked up the front steps and crossed the porch. She had always dreaded going to her grandmother's house because her grandmother was a thick white-haired Irish woman who could see right through your skin. She would look at Elizabeth, and Elizabeth was certain her grandmother knew every bad thought and bad deed she had ever committed. Her grandmother's hands were stubby and coarse from years of hard work. Her face was creased with age, and all who knew her would have to agree that very few of the lines could be attributed to laugh lines. Life was serious for her grandmother. That was, perhaps, where Elizabeth inherited her dark side. Only, unlike Elizabeth, her grandmother's seriousness was the burden of being good, proper, and grateful to God for her blessings. Now, tonight, Elizabeth needed to understand that fierce faith that had steeled her grandmother and frightened Elizabeth.

Gram's house was old. It smelled of the age of everything: her sofa, the wallpaper, the pictures on the wall. Her grandmother was a fanatical housecleaner, but there was just no way to clean away old. Gram had no patience for throwing out anything with a speck of worth left in it. She patched and glued and covered the worn parts of everything. And being a hard worker, she was not worried about the details of her repairs. Clean was enough. Her patches did not have to be perfect, the glued cracks were okay to be seen, and when a hole couldn't be repaired, she just threw a doily over it and moved on. But still, despite her fear of her grandmother, Elizabeth believed her grandmother was the only person who could help her.

Elizabeth dropped her backpack by the door and walked into the dim room. Her grandmother was sitting in her rocking chair by the lamp table. There was a picture of a weeping willow tree on the table that her youngest son had drawn for her before he had died of scarlet fever when he was only five. Her Bible was open faceup on the table, where she had been reading it.

"Here," Gram said, "pull over that hassock, and we can talk."

Elizabeth brought the threadbare brown hassock in front of her grandmother and sat down on it. "I want to know about God. And Jesus. And angels if you know anything about them."

Her grandmother laughed. She laughed out loud, and Elizabeth liked the sound of it. "That is a lot to answer. I'm old. I may not have the time to tell you everything I believe about God and Jesus and angels, but I will tell you that what I am about to share is the greatest story ever told. No one but God could bring us such a perfect story."

So her grandmother explained Genesis. "God made this world for man to enjoy. Because our happiness is His happiness. But man is not godlike. He is human, and being human is what happened that ruined the perfect world God made for us. He was patient and impatient with man. He spoke personally to a few men and tried to guide His creation back to their promised land. But man has always been difficult. Now, in time you and I can go through the stories of Abraham and Jonas and David and all the rest, but tonight let's get right to the best part. All the chosen ones before Jesus foretold of a Savior. Everything in the Old Testament happened so we would be brought to the moment of Jesus's birth. I mean, can you imagine a more perfect plan than to have the Son of God born to experience our lives, to feel our worries and pains and understand what it really meant to be one of our Father's creations? Who better to save man than someone who was godly but knew, firsthand, our human frailties?"

Elizabeth thought about that. "That would be perfect if we hadn't crucified Him. I mean if Jesus and God could have just talked, then why couldn't they figure out how to save us from ourselves? Instead God let His Son be tortured. That has always bothered me, Gram. I never liked to look at Jesus on the cross, just hanging there so helpless like that. It felt like something was terribly wrong with God rather than right."

Gram sat back and nodded. "I can see that. But you are thinking like a human, and Jesus and his Father are God. Jesus knew what His destiny was. That was why He tried to warn His disciples and why He didn't resist His capture and death. He accepted being tortured in the cruelest and lowliest manner of that day so He could free us of our sins.

Remember, before this, man was not allowed to speak directly to God. If you needed to clear your soul or ask God for something, you had to go to a rabbi, who was the only one worthy of speaking directly to God. After Jesus's death, the curtain between God and man tore apart, and now we have direct access to speak to God ourselves."

"I'm still confused. If God wanted us to be able to speak directly to Him, then why didn't He just do it without Jesus? I mean, He is God. He can do anything?"

"God gave man free will when He created him. He gave us rules, but also the free will to obey them or not. So of course, things were going to get out of control. Most humans I know are not smart enough to figure out the big picture here. So say, if Jesus had come and walked among us, if He had taught what God wanted us to know, how God wanted us to love and take care of each other, then would man really have been convinced enough to change his ways and do what was right and good and, for all time, make the decision to always obey God's laws?"

"Still," Elizabeth said, "there had to be another way than what happened. Couldn't God just let Jesus live and teach and perform enough miracles to convince us that He was really the Son of God and we needed to listen to Him? Why did He have to die the way He did?"

"Oh," Gram said with a big smile, "that is the best part. The most brilliant part. Think of it, if Jesus had walked the earth, teaching and healing and then dying, say, in His sleep when He was really old, then how would that have changed man? We knew the rules. God had written them out for us on stone, for pity's sake, and still we went on breaking them. Jesus could have retold us the rules, He could have been one of the greatest examples of how God wanted us to live, but we were still human. We would have written about Him, maybe, had holidays honoring Him, but His story wouldn't have changed the world."

Elizabeth frowned, still not quite getting it.

"Think of one of your books. Would you think it was a great story if your hero died in the middle of the book and in the worst way imaginable? If he was the promise of salvation for the earth, and then he let himself purposely get caught and didn't even try to defend himself or escape, all the while knowing his gruesome fate?"

"I doubt it would have been published," Elizabeth said, still frowning.

"Exactly, and yet that is what happened in the greatest story ever told. Jesus knew, He accepted the assignment, He walked the dusty road for three years in total poverty, all the while changing lives, healing, and forgiving and loving the worst of the worst. He, as you say, walked the talk. Then He died, refusing anything to numb the pain, accepting the full atonement for man's sins, and worst of all, separated from God because of man's sins. He suffered it all for us. How more beautiful can that get?"

"I'm still missing something," Elizabeth said. "He walked in such a small area of the world, He healed people no one really cared about, He never became like a great leader whom anyone feared. How did His story change the world?"

"Because He was resurrected just as He had said He would be. He came back and walked the earth and proved He was the way to life everlasting. And you are right, the story could have ended there, except that for the first time, man had actually lived with God, they had walked beside Him, they had eaten with Him, they had witnessed His miracles. His followers believed in Him so completely that they went out to the corners of the world, and with the Holy Spirit inside them, they spread His promise that God loves us and death would never be the end."

Elizabeth sat back and shook her head. "The Holy Spirit? This is getting interesting."

Gram nodded. "Cookie break. And then I will take questions."

Elizabeth got up from the hassock and followed her shuffling little grandmother into the kitchen. She wondered now why she had ever been intimidated by her. "There is just one question that can't wait," Elizabeth said. "Why didn't you ever tell me all this before?"

Gram unscrewed the cap of the round glass cookie jar and the aroma of oatmeal cookies trickled out. "Were you ready before?"

Elizabeth thought about that. She knew she should have wanted it, she knew she was searching for something in her dark period, but no, Gram was right, believing in God wouldn't have been an option before. Before the painting class that released something softer hidden in her each time she walked into the studio. She would bring Gram to see her painting of the angel. It all made sense now when before today, before Daniel told his story, she didn't know why she had painted any of it. But she would go back now and paint angels in all her dark rooms.

"One or two cookies," Gram asked.

"Oh, two," Elizabeth replied then remembered to add, "please."

Ruthie worked the morning shift at the diner two days a week. She worked at the Bar & Grill four nights a week. Nights were her best as she was definitely not a morning person, which only, she'd modestly admit, testified to her great waitressing talent of hiding her bad morning mood from the customers. Of course, the more cheerful the chatter, the brighter the sarcasm, the better the tip. It was all about presentation, and she was queen of presenting whatever it took.

"Hey," cheap Raymond called out to her. "My toast is cold."

Ruthie sashayed over to his booth. She sighed and started to educate him on the reality that toast assumed room temperature almost before you even finished the buttering. She wanted to tell him to get off his lazy, good-for-nothing, government-supported ass and go home and make his own toast. After all, what was the sense of catering to his selfishness when he stiffed her on her tip and there were other customers more deserving of her service than he was? But she didn't say it. She looked down at his leathery face and his dirty fingernails, and she changed her mind. She reached down and grabbed up his toast.

"I'll just get right back to the kitchen and warm this up for you," she said. That made her laugh, thinking of warming a piece of toast and then hustling it back to the table before it could cool off. *Yeah,* she thought, *being nice could be fun.* And maybe her guardian angel was watching and would report back to God—new thought, but one she couldn't afford to dismiss in case it was real.

Raymond appeared satisfied with her promise, so she went back to the pass-through and handed the toast back to the confused cook. "A new piece of toast. I'll wait here for it," she said.

"What's wrong with this one?"

Ruthie shrugged. "Raymond didn't like it."

The cook threw it into the trash and grumbled that he didn't have time for this crap. Ruthie stuck a saucer under the warming light and waited for the new toast. This was actually as good as a tip—well, almost. She might forget what a pain in the ass Raymond was and remember this little trick of warming the toast plate. Yes, she had other good tippers, who might actually appreciate this little extra attention to their dining pleasure.

She carried the warm toast plate back to Raymond and sat it down. "Now get on that quickly before it cools down," she told Raymond. "Cook doesn't want to see me back at his window with a cold piece of toast again."

Raymond picked up the toast with one eye on her. He was suddenly worried that Ruthie might have put something unsavory on his toast as payback for complaining. She was not acting like her usual self. She hadn't even given him a dirty look all morning.

Ruthie winked at him and swirled around to refill Ms. Sally's coffee. She hoped this good feeling about herself lasted until her shift was over. That was as much as God should expect for one day. After all, this was all new to her.

She had thought about it all night. She believed in signs. A shooting star for good luck. A rainbow just when you were thinking of giving up and accepting your crappy life was as good as it was ever going to be. A woman wearing a red scarf right next to the red purses when she was trying to decide which color of shoes to match with her psychedelic pants. And now angels. How could you argue with an angel?

Of course, the angel wasn't actually her sign. It was Twilight's. And apparently, Daniel's too. They both were responsible for answering to whatever was needed there. But still, Daniel's story had made her open to the possibility that God might be aware of her, so she had better clean up her act. She was not only far from being unacceptable to God but also just as far from actually being acceptable to him. What could it hurt to try a little harder to move in the right direction? Maybe after the painting classes ended, she could volunteer that time to some worthy cause. Really rack up some good points. Just in case.

———〜∞∞∞∞〜———

Milly left at one o'clock sharp. She had lunch with Fran and then cleaned the kitchen before she loaded her battered old suitcase into her trunk and drove off without a backward glance.

Good riddance, Fran thought as she peered out the window. Like as not, Milly would get herself lost before she even got halfway there. Fran would probably get a phone call right in the middle of *Wheel of Fortune* from Milly's spineless son inquiring where his mother was. Fran shook her head at the thought. They all deserved one another.

Fran wandered around the house a little. It was too early to watch TV. She didn't want to turn into a couch potato. It was too early to pour her first glass of wine. She was too wide awake to take a nap. Maybe she'd just go out on the front porch and sit awhile in the swing, just relax now that she had time to herself. She had forgotten what that was like. Since Milly's husband had died of cancer and Fran, being such a good heart, had invited Milly to move in with her, Fran's life had never been the same. Milly and Bert had lived in a trailer, for heaven's sake, so of course, Milly was grateful to find herself in Fran's nice house. Milly was all helpful and pleasant at first. Then over the years she had turned back into the nervous, irritating mess she had been as a child.

Yes, Fran thought as she swung back and forth, catching a slight breeze, she could get used to this again. She had never been one to need anything or anyone. This week could be just what the doctor ordered.

Fran swung contentedly, noticing who drove past, who picked up their mail, and who needed to paint their house . . . until Eleanor came out to water the geraniums by her front steps. Then Fran scraped her feet on the porch slats to stop the swing. She stood up and scurried down to the sidewalk. "I saw you got home pretty late last night," she called across the street.

Eleanor looked up from her watering. "Really. It didn't seem very late to me."

"Well, I meant considering you were a woman out alone at night."

Eleanor forced a smile. "Yes. Thankfully, I made it safely."

"You've got something special on Tuesday night?"

"Painting class."

"I see. Well, that's good, I suppose," Fran said. Then she thought a moment. "But I could have sworn you stopped them when Bill died."

"I restarted them."

"Good. Good for you. Best to get back up on the horse."

Eleanor emptied the water pitcher and turned to go back inside, then hesitated and turned back to Fran. "Do you read the Bible, Fran?"

Fran pulled in her chin. "What? Read the Bible? Well, certainly, I have. I mean not at the moment, but I did when I was younger."

"Did you get it?"

"Get what?"

"You know," Eleanor said, walking across the road to Fran's sidewalk. "Did you understand it?"

"Certainly. I've never had a problem with comprehension."

"Good, because I was trying to read it this morning, and frankly, all the sacrificing and blood smearing and killing . . . well, I didn't expect that in the Bible. I mean not so much. I don't know why God wants us to know all that to be able to believe in Him."

Fran nodded seriously. "There was a lot of that way back then."

"I guess if I keep reading, He will explain it. The Bible is His word. I'm sure it will eventually make sense to me."

"Yes, that's the secret. Just keep working at it. But," Fran asked, "why are you reading it? You going to church now?"

"I'm thinking of it."

"Joining things is good. I used to belong to the Ladies Auxiliary at the Elks club. I was in it because my husband had been in it. After a while, though, I just got burned out. They expected me to run everything, and then there was backstabbing and the like. It was just not worth it."

"Sorry to hear that."

"But go where you think you should. If church is for you, then do it. Just don't expect it to be some instant cure-all. We, unfortunately, have to deal with our problems on our own. Painting classes and church are good diversions, but just getting on with our life is the most we can actually aim for. Mark my word, there is no magic pill out there to set things back the way they were."

"I suppose not," Eleanor said, realizing now what a dunce she was to even try to talk to this woman. Fran, of all people, would never get the message of anything she hadn't created herself. Fran's interpretation of the Bible was actually something Eleanor didn't even want to think about.

"There is one thing I remember about the Bible," Fran said thoughtfully. "All that blood smearing and sacrificing, well, that was how the people back in biblical times practiced religion. That's because they felt they were giving something worthy to God, because they were told they weren't worthy enough as just themselves. Also strict rules and harsh punishments were necessary because they were just barbarians. Anyway, that was in the old part. In the new part, I remember my father saying something like Jesus was the pure sacrificial lamb that shed His blood so no one had to do that messy part again. He ended it. Jesus started a whole new way of doing religion."

"Well, I'm grateful for that."

"Yeah." Fran chuckled. "You won't have to go out and rustle up a lamb if you decide to go to church on Sunday. Money is all it takes today."

"Good to know," Eleanor said.

"Oh, and one more thing," Fran said. "Sit in the back of the church. That way, if you get bored and want to sneak out, practically no one will see."

"Thanks," Eleanor said and scurried across the road before Fran thought of anything else. She did have to admit, though, Fran's way of looking at things did sort of make going to church a little less daunting. And maybe she would just skip to the new part of the Bible for now. In fact, she already felt more comfortable just thinking about Jesus. People might not know the stories behind the Old Testament names, but Jesus's story had been with them their whole life. Every schoolchild got Christmas and Easter off, so church or not, Jesus was a familiar face and important figure since kindergarten.

Eleanor made it nearly to her door before she heard Fran yell across the street that she had noticed the cucumbers in Bill's garden were starting to go soft. She'd be glad to come and get some for pickling if Eleanor didn't mind sharing.

Daniel had a couple of books set beside his cash register in case Twilight came by and still wanted them. One was written by a famous neurosurgeon who had traveled to heaven and back while in a coma. The beauty of this book, Daniel thought, was that if one was trying to decide if they could believe such an experience or not, this doctor had never believed his patients or their family members when they had related such tales to him. He had been certain they were either medication-induced hallucinations or wistful dreams. But when it had happened to him personally, and he had scoured through every medical detail of his care, he had to believe it had really happened. So he had finally written it in a book to help others. Of course, very few people would be familiar with the book because that was not the type of fantasy reading they were looking for. And in all honesty, Daniel himself would not have purchased such a book before he needed desperately to believe it.

The other book was written by a hospice nurse who had witnessed many varied and miraculous death experiences. Daniel could see Twilight being touched by those stories. Daniel still wasn't completely certain he should have shared his story with everyone last night. If felt wrong to deny them when they wanted to stay, but then these women could never have suspected what they were asking to hear.

Daniel walked around the counter and was going to step outside for some fresh air—his own company could get claustrophobic—when the door to his shop opened and Doris brushed in. Her smile was weak and her makeup, a little rushed.

"You busy?" she asked, snapping her head to survey the store.

"All is under control at the moment."

"Good. Good. We can talk, then."

"Sure. Of course."

Doris paused and caught her breath. Where to begin? Best to get right to it. "I've been an excellent wife to an ungrateful and unworthy slug for forty years. As you can imagine, I had my choice of any man in town, and yet... do you believe in the devil? Yes, yes, of course, you do. If you believe in God, then you have to believe in the devil. Well, anyway, whoever, the devil or witchcraft or something in that vein, must have had control of my senses, because I picked Frederick. Seriously, he may be successful at a lot of things, but doing right by his wife has never been one of them."

"Please," Daniel said, holding up his hand to stop her. "I'm not a marriage counselor. This type of help is not what I am good at. Trust me."

"Well, who, then, do you suggest I talk to? Everyone in this town knows me. Knows Frederick. And even if there was someone I wanted to tell, I could never trust anyone in this town to keep it to themselves. No, you are the only one."

"What about your minister? They are sworn to keep confidences . . . confident."

"No. No. Out of the question. Rev. Williams is wonderful, but he is, unfortunately, one of those reverends who has never married. I mean he could have and hasn't. So anyway, what would he know? But you, you knew how to be a husband. You seem to be very discreet, not one to get a thrill out of exposing others' dirty laundry. I trust you. And you were married. And you were a wonderful, loving husband, and I . . ."

"Wait. There is no way you can know what kind of husband I was. And even if I had been as wonderful and loving as you think, I know nothing about giving marriage advice. Seriously, I made my mistakes. I have my regrets. I just know about art and minding my own business."

Doris sat back on her heels as though Daniel's refusal of help had physically pushed her. "I just had the most horrible night of my life, and there is no one to turn to." She felt a tear and brushed at it.

"I'm sorry," Daniel said.

"Apparently not," she said. "I have never felt as alone and vulnerable in my life, and I have no one to even talk to." She shook her head sadly.

"If you don't expect me to actually be able to solve your problems, then, if you just need to talk to someone, I am a very good listener. Marriage does, to some personality types, foster the skill of listening."

Doris wasn't sure. What good would just listening to her do? She could have talked to the wall at home if she just needed to talk. "I don't know," she said, shaking her head.

"How about I close up shop? Wednesday mornings are always slow. We can go somewhere, get a cup of coffee, and see if we can think of anything to help you."

"Really? That would be nice. But we can't talk in public. Seriously, you have no idea how many busybodies would love to know my personal business."

"I'm certain there are many," Daniel said and turned to hide his smile and get his keys from the hook behind the counter. Doris was the one woman he had not invited to join the painting class. For one thing, she never needed an invitation to do what she wanted, and the other thing was that, well, he hadn't seen a need in her. He was frankly surprised to see her needing or even asking for advice now unless . . . this drama was for another purpose altogether. Doris was definitely a slippery slope, but what could he do?

"I know," Doris said, brightening, taking control again. "We can go to the Rotary Hall. They don't do anything on Wednesdays. We can pick up coffee to go at the diner or the counter at the drugstore. Maybe even a pastry. I was too upset to eat breakfast, and now I can feel my blood sugar dropping."

"Are you a diabetic?" Daniel asked.

"Oh lord, no. But you can tell when your body isn't functioning properly. Skipping meals isn't healthy. Everyone knows that. How we take care of our temple determines everything?"

"Yes, yes, it does," Daniel said, following Doris out and locking the shop door. So coffee and a sugary pastry?

They were seated at the receptionist desk in the Rotary Hall with their coffees and a glazed bear claw and two blueberry muffins.

"Help yourself," Doris said, slurping her hot coffee and picking up the bear claw. She chuckled. "Did you see how everyone in the diner stared at us together?"

"Did that bother you?"

"Good lord, no. Well, I do wish I had taken a little more time with my makeup, but who cares if any of those people run back to Frederick with big stories?" She stopped chewing for a moment then sat her bear claw down. "Frederick wouldn't care no matter what anyone told him."

"Has he always been like that?" Daniel asked to try and lead her in a positive direction, maybe remind her when she believed Frederick didn't feel like that, and then they could examine why he had changed.

"Yes, I'm afraid so. And at first I liked the challenge of getting his attention, but it has worn thin, you know? I don't want to try anymore. I don't want to waste my life caring if he notices me." She sat her coffee down. "And now that I realize that his approval isn't necessary, I don't know what to replace him with. Whom do I have to keep a nice home for, to organize amazing dinner parties for, to exercise and stay beautiful for? It's like I wasted my life. Frederick has robbed me of a happy life."

"I understand," Daniel said.

Doris frowned and looked at him. Hadn't he implied that his marriage had been wonderful? Certainly, Jill had filled his life with mutual affection instead of leaving it lacking and loveless and virtually empty. Then sadly, of course, she had died and left him alone. But at least, he had good memories to grieve over. What did Doris have but disappointments? "So anyway," Doris said, "how did you find your way back? How did you get on with a purpose? I have no purpose!"

"It took a while. I wallowed and stumbled and suffered. But eventually, because she had left me with something even though I didn't realize it at first, she had left me with the knowledge that she was somewhere. That I would see her again when I was finished fulfilling whatever God's purpose was for me. So I guess when I realized that, when I grasped that I still had a reason to live, that's when I began to read, to understand, and to believe, it changed me. God has changed me."

"Yes. God. Well, unfortunately, he hasn't sent any angels to visit me so I don't know what to do now. Do I divorce Frederick? I mean, he hasn't done anything I could really point to in court, but that's the problem, isn't it? He just hasn't done anything. It's like I've lived my life alone." She sighed and picked up her bear claw.

"Have you talked to him about this?"

"What?" Doris glanced at Daniel. She had been still thinking about divorcing Frederick. "Oh, talk to him? No. No. There would be no point in that. He's happy. He wouldn't understand. Of course, I did lock him out of our room last night."

"That may have opened up a place to start a dialogue," Daniel said.

Doris shook her head. "No. He just slept in the guest room without a fuss and didn't even check the door again. He was gone when I came downstairs, so I guess it was all okay with him."

"I think it wouldn't hurt to, maybe, talk to your minister."

"I know you trust all that. And I do go to church, but that really doesn't have anything to do with my real life. I need to just divorce him, get it over with, and find someone who wants me. Let's face it, I'm not getting any younger."

"Do you have any children?"

"Just a son. He lives in California—San Francisco, actually. He has a great job. Travels a lot," Doris said, "but unfortunately, he married way beneath himself. I mean his wife is well educated, but she is no beauty. Eric is a handsome man. He could have done so much better."

"Do they come back to visit? Or do you go there?"

"They come back every few years. His family is growing, and they are very busy. And as for going there, no, Frederick is content to sit in this dreary place and not travel any farther than to his hunting camp. Though he'd hate me to tell anyone this, I believe he won't travel because he is afraid of flying." She looked at Daniel and nodded. "Really. I'm a prisoner. I've tried to make the best of my situation, but suddenly, I can't ignore it any longer, I'm wasting away. I've lived for Frederick, and he has robbed me of all the opportunities I should have had. The places I should have gone. The happiness I deserved."

"I would never have guessed," Daniel said.

"Right. I know. No one would, and that's what has been so difficult about being me. I could never let my disappointment show. So much was expected of me. It's been hard."

"Maybe you just need a vacation. Just to get away and reevaluate everything. Your church has retreats that could help you. No one has to feel alone."

"Oh, Daniel, seriously? The church? I had no idea you were such a God fanatic. I'm not talking life-and-death. I'm talking about real problems. Real heartache. I thought you would be more sensitive to that. You are an artist. You are supposed to feel deeper and see more. I thought you would be able to give me advice on what to do to be as . . . well, contented as you. I am crippled with sadness here, and you . . . you always seem at such peace. I want peace. I want to stop trying and stop being so disappointed."

"Then do it. Just stop trying."

Doris thought about that. "And do what instead?"

"There are lots of things to do to feel good. I saw a flyer that your church is having a garage sale this coming weekend. Certainly, you would have things to donate."

"Of course, I have nice things. But my things are too good for those type of people. I mean, how could I see just anyone in town parading around in my clothes? That would be humiliating."

"I don't know, Doris, I warned you I couldn't give you advice. What do I know about your life?"

"Fine, fine," Doris said. "I'll figure this out by myself. But while we are already here, I'd like to go over some ideas I had for the art show. After we were here the other night, the ideas have just been flooding in. Oh, and when we were figuring out where to set up each person's exhibit, we didn't pick your area. Aren't you showing any of your paintings?"

"No. This isn't about me."

"But it should be. I mean where were any of us before you came?"

Unfortunately, some of you will still be in the same place when I leave, Daniel thought. "My paintings are on display in the shop."

"Not all of them," Doris said, and then slyly, because he was all wrapped up in this God thing since his story last night, she added, "Maybe you have some religious paintings you would like to display. We can set them up beside Twilight's. Don't you have some with angels and God and lightning bolts?"

"No. I just paint everyday miracles."

"Really? Like what?"

"Like everything you've seen that I have painted."

Doris scowled. "I've never seen any miracles in your paintings. They are just people and trees and clouds and maybe deer."

"Exactly," Daniel said. "Now what are we doing about the lighting in here? Some of the paintings will show better with a soft, direct light on them."

"Or some like mine would be better in the dark," Doris said and then laughed at her own humility.

———⁂———

Elizabeth woke up with the sun pouring in her grandmother's window. Gram's side of the bed was empty, and Elizabeth could hear rustling sounds from the kitchen. They had talked and talked and talked and then decided to sleep together so they could keep talking. She had not slept with anyone ever. She was not one to sneak into her parents' bed if she heard thunder or had a nightmare. And as Gram lived in town, there had never been a need to spend the night. Elizabeth had liked the softness of Gram's feather bed and the faint smell of her grandmother's lilac powder. Of course, she was self-conscious at first. Gram had other bedrooms. But when they had gotten into their nightgowns and brushed their teeth and cleansed their faces, Gram had suggested they get snuggled in, and she would tell Elizabeth the story of Moses. Elizabeth was surprised when Gram finished. Why would God pick such imperfect humans to lead his people? First there was Abraham who had followed God's word blindly, sitting for years, waiting. And then after sending one son into the wilderness, never knowing if he lived or died, he was then willing to sacrifice his other son, if God hadn't stopped him. And now here was Moses hiding out to save himself from the Egyptians, and really, he wasn't all that articulate. He didn't even want God's assignment when he was actually spoken to by God directly. How could anyone think of not listening to that? Elizabeth shook her head. There was just so much to know, so much to understand. Gram had said that it would all fit together when they were finished. God had put all the right stuff in there, and it would turn out to be the greatest story man would ever receive.

Elizabeth got out of bed and changed into her clothes. She made the bed up and stopped by the bathroom on her way downstairs. Her hair was a little scary in the morning, but Gram wasn't easily startled.

Gram looked up when Elizabeth came into the kitchen. "Good morning. You ready for blueberry pancakes?"

Elizabeth nodded. "They smell wonderful. Can I help with anything?"

Gram paused, her hand ready to pour another circle of batter onto the hot skillet. "You can help me understand you," she said gently, more gentle and pleading than Elizabeth had ever heard from her grandmother.

"What do you mean?"

"What are you so afraid of or so sad about that you have to hide yourself? Granted, you have always been a serious child, but I remember how, when you were little, you loved to color and draw things. And those pictures were happy and colorful. I saved many of them. But then, you withdrew, and everything about you was dark. It broke my heart to lose that sweet little girl. I've wanted to ask you this before, but you were so closed up I never felt I should try to ask you anything. Now, it seems we can talk. God has answered my prayers."

"You prayed for me?"

"You're my only grandchild. What could be more important than you?"

Elizabeth felt like retreating, but she had to know. "What . . . what did you ask Him for?"

Gram flipped the pancakes and pulled the warming plate from the oven. "That He would help you to find your way back. You're a good girl. I knew one day He would touch you."

Elizabeth sank down into the chair. "I want to know about Him, but I don't think I am ready for Him to know about me. Something happened to me yesterday that I don't understand. It frightens me."

Gram set the warm plate of pancakes and bacon on the table. She sat down in her chair next to Elizabeth and took her granddaughter's hand. It was thin and helpless. "He knew you before you were born. There is no escaping His love for you. But I understand. It has taken me years to know all that we talked about last night. Years to cross the line from wanting to believe to believing. That is where you are. I know it, and God knows it. So relax. Take your time. Here, eat your breakfast. Blueberries and warm maple syrup always make everything feel better."

Elizabeth withdrew her hand and picked up her butter knife. "I have never fit in. I mean I knew it even before I decided to just give up and accept that I was different. Actually, I didn't even want to be like the other kids, but it still hurt when I wasn't. I know that doesn't make any sense. But somehow I actually felt better when I just decided to stop caring. I felt safe being nearly invisible in the shadows. Everyone stayed away from me because they saw I didn't want to be like them. That was easier."

"Oh my," Gram said.

"But now, if I believe in God and they know it, well, it will just make me even stranger to them. God is forbidden in school, and no one that I know really talks about Him. I guess I can believe but hide it like I have hidden everything else. Right?"

Gram shook her head. "Wrong. There will always be people who don't want to believe and, therefore, want to take away your right to believe. But we must be true to ourselves, Elizabeth. It is time for you to come out of hiding and accept yourself as God made you. Whatever you think is different about you is exactly how you were intended to be."

Elizabeth thought about that. "I like that," she said.

They both ate blueberry pancakes and bacon quietly, then Gram asked Elizabeth what it was exactly that she thought was so different about herself.

"Well, I guess, when I first realized that I didn't like to play like the other kids. I didn't want to pretend dolls were real or be chased or . . . make myself giggle and act silly like the other girls. I didn't understand the boys at all, and the girls wanted to be princesses or mothers or, I don't know, just not themselves. I didn't know how to think like I was someone else. I accepted that I felt better when I was by myself. I liked quiet things. I liked to read. I read everywhere I went. It kept me safe. I liked working on things by myself. One time I made this whole miniature village just like in my book. Every day I couldn't wait to get home and work on it. I made it out of paper. Little paper boxes decorated like I thought they would be in the real village. But then when it was finished, I realized that there was no one to share it with. No one would care about my paper village or understand why it was important for me to make it. Honestly, I couldn't even think of anyone I would even want to share it with. I mean, not one person. That's when I realized that I was alone and that I had put myself there because I wasn't like other people." Elizabeth sighed and stopped talking.

"Goodness," Gram said. "You have certainly been hard on yourself. But the good news is that I was like you, and I would say that I have turned out all right." Gram smiled and patted Elizabeth's hand. "Accept yourself, and the world will accept you."

"How did you do it?"

"I was twelve, actually. My mother and I always fought about me wearing dresses. I had two older brothers, and Mom wanted me to be her little girl and not a tomboy. But I didn't like dresses. You couldn't climb trees in dresses or work in the dirt in the garden. I loved the garden." Gram chuckled. "Guess I still do, but I have learned how to work it in a dress. Anyway, when I was twelve, my mother died. Just like that. So sudden it is still hard to believe. I put a dress on that day and have never worn anything else. I know why I did it, I hoped my mother would know somehow and be pleased. But more than that, I kept wearing them because I realized that I could still be myself wearing anything. I still tramped though the fields, still climbed over stonewalls, still fought with my brothers. I accepted I was a tomboy in a dress. And now you have to accept that you are a sensitive, quiet person in a loud and sometimes unkind world. You are not wrong. You are not different. You are exactly who you were made to be."

Elizabeth sat still for a moment, picking at her thumbnail. "I'm sorry about your mother."

Gram nodded. "God has his reasons."

"Do you believe that?"

"I do."

"Even..." Elizabeth said, hardly daring to mention more pain, but she had to know. "Even when Edward died so young?"

"Yes, I've been tested, to be certain, but there is no middle ground. You believe, or you don't. And I believe that God's plan is more important than mine."

"Do you think he has a plan for me?"

"Most definitely," Gram said. "Most definitely. Now scat and get ready for school."

Chapter 4

Ruthie usually napped between her diner and the Bar & Grill shifts, but today she couldn't. Max was at the gravel pit, working, so she had the apartment to herself. It was quiet, which usually worked for her, but today the quiet was too loud to relax. All she could think about as she stretched out on the unmade bed was how there was no noise in her life. She felt like Twilight's paintings before the light was added—like a black hole with all the substance sucked out. Ruthie sat up, drawing her legs to her and hugging her knees. Maybe it was time to move on again, maybe do things differently this time, like . . . like? Maybe she could call Robert and see if it was okay to just see the girls for a few minutes, maybe meet them in a park, and she could bring picnic things. Maybe they would tell her about their lives, and she could just look at them as they talked. That's all she wanted—to just look at them. She wasn't a bad person. She had tried in her limited way to stay in touch with them. She had sent them gifts for their birthdays but had never gotten a reply if they had even received them. What kind of manners was Robert teaching them?

No. No. She couldn't do that. The last time she had tried seeing them, it had ended horribly, and she had agreed with Robert that she wouldn't try again until the girls were old enough to ask to see her. He'd told her she couldn't just swoop in and out of their lives as though it did no damage. "You made your choice," he had said. "Now live with it. For once, Ruth, do the unselfish thing."

And that was why she had to leave Robert. He was always saying that crap. So she wasn't Ms. Mommy Homemaker. She wasn't fulfilled by catering to the constant demands of everyone else's needs. She wasn't the kind of mother who woke up at six to pour cereal in a bowl when she had been up most of the night finishing a good book. Why had she been expected to be the only unselfish one?

Ruthie swung her legs over the edge of the bed and sat there for a while. She hated going to work without a nap. It was hard enough to paste a smile on when she actually felt happy enough to be there, but when she was tired, it was a struggle. Still she could do it. She was a professional.

Ruthie got up and went to the dresser. She fished around behind her underwear and drew out her teak box with butterflies carved into it. She opened it and counted her money. She contributed to the apartment bills; she had never been a schmoozer, but she was also a hoarder. She rested better when she knew she had a comfortable stash in her secret place. Some of the men she had lived with could not be trusted when it came to money, hers or anyone's, but Max was okay. He was a giver more than a taker. That's why she had stayed with him so long—well, longer than the others. Regardless, she had enough money to move on, to pack her meager belongings into the back of her old red Plymouth Barracuda, and to rattle off to someplace new. Maybe she'd ask around the barflies tonight, see where they had been or where they had come from, and get some interesting ideas. Maybe Max would want to come too. They could go to Barbados, maybe. One of her regulars always talked of going to Barbados. He had never been there, but the fact that he always dreamed of it was intriguing enough. Or maybe she could just go back to Linton. She wouldn't tell Robert or the girls that she was there, but there was a chance they might just bump into her at some random time and place, and it would be harmless. She wouldn't be there to impose. She was a free person. The divorce papers did not state that she could never live in the same town again. The girls were teenagers now. Certainly, they weren't so fragile that just seeing their mother on the street would damage them. I mean, look at the things teenagers deal with today.

Ruthie got up and headed for the shower. She paused to turn on some music; the quiet was driving her nuts. She grabbed her work clothes and then paused and thought of her painting. Huh. Strange that she would think of that. Maybe she would wait until after the art show. Maybe she would even send a note to Robert and the girls and invite them to come see her work. It was certainly not great art, but it was one thing since the birth of her girls that she had pulled from herself that she actually felt good about.

⸺∿⦚∾⟡∾⦚∿⸺

Pauline rummaged through the boxes in the attic until she found her old paints and canvases. She held up one finished painting and grimaced. It was awful, actually—a clumsy attempt at copying the front of a Christmas card. The snow was flat. Any self-respecting red cardinal would have been heartsick to see how it had been portrayed. The evergreen branch it sat on looked like a toilet brush. Pauline couldn't contain herself. She had to laugh or cry. She laughed and put the canvas back into the box. Why had she fostered, for all these years, the dream that she could paint when this disaster was what she had produced?

Pauline fished out a charcoal pencil and a blank canvas. She started drawing swirls—just a canvas of swirls. She liked it. She could see what it would look like if the background were, say, a blue and burgundy mix, the colors mingling so there were no distinct boundaries. Then add tiny dots of white here and there—blurry dots, not circles. Then she would paint the swirls white and gray, depending on the angle of the light. It would be so freeing and whimsical, yet if you stared at it long enough, it would be something else—something serious and pretty.

"Mom, where are you?"

Pauline dropped her pencil and canvas back into the box. "Coming," she called out. She pushed herself up and headed for the attic stairs. There was just never enough time anymore. She was behind on her housework. The kids were going to school without their homework checked. The evening meal was more processed than fresh. She hoped that the time spent painting and working in the art shop hadn't been a mistake. Maybe her art wasn't worth the sacrifice.

Pauline hurried down the steps, thinking of the art show. She was excited and frightened to show her work. Daniel had complimented it. He knew art and said he saw something in her finished pieces. She was—she would have to admit—becoming obsessed. She would think about the painting when she wasn't working on it. She couldn't wait to get back to it and add or change the little things she thought of that would bring it to life.

Jennifer and Jeffrey, her twins, were waiting at the bottom of the stairs, looking up at her with their freckly round faces.

"What were you looking for?" Jennifer asked.

"Oh, nothing special. How was your day?"

"Okay, I guess. Do I have to go to dance class tonight?"

Jeffrey had wandered off to get something to snack on. Pauline told him they were out of fruit, but he could have a granola bar. He said he wanted potato chips. Pauline just shook her head and turned back to Jennifer.

"How come you never let me have potato chips for a snack?" Jennifer whined.

"Why don't you want to go to dance class?"

Jennifer walked over and grabbed a fistful of potato chips from the bag before Jeffrey could pull it away. Her hand was so full that some of the chips tumbled out onto the floor and got crushed as the two scrapped over the bag of chips.

Pauline walked over and grabbed the bag from Jeffrey. "Get a granola bar, and go start your homework." Then she added "Now!" for emphasis. The two pulled back and looked at her. Who was this? Their mother had always been calm and fair and accommodating. She would have taken the time to explain the negative properties of chips over granola and cajoled them into what they should have.

Jennifer began to sniffle, and Pauline told her to get into her leotard.

"I'm telling Daddy how mean you are," Jennifer threatened as she hurried from the kitchen.

Pauline stuffed the bag of chips into the trash and then straightened and drew in a deep breath. She wanted to paint, but she was taking Jennifer to dance class and then coming home and preparing dinner. She went to the hall closet to get the broom then stopped. She had to paint that canvas in the attic. She had to. She would start it as soon as she got home from dropping off Jennifer, and then she'd call Tim and have him pick up pizza after he picked up Jennifer from dance. It was time to come out into the open. She had felt like some kind of drug addict who had to hide her habit. Tim and the kids might not understand her painting, they might resent the time she took from them to paint, but the bottom line was that she had waited long enough to answer the call. Something in her had broken free, and she wasn't going to stuff it back in. She grabbed the broom and danced with it back into the kitchen to sweep up the crumbs.

Doris lit all the candles in the dining room. She dimmed the chandelier so that the room was bathed in an amber light. She went to the table and fussed with the arrangement of gold-and-orange flowers she had picked up on her way home from her meeting with Daniel. Of course, Daniel had been no help—God this and God that. Well, he had suggested that she just stop trying, and that had, inadvertently, sparked her new plan. She wouldn't stop trying. That wasn't her style. What she would do, what her plan was, was to lure Frederick back and then slap him with divorce papers. She had an appointment with an attorney tomorrow—an out-of-town attorney, of course, so no one would suspect what she was planning.

The music she had selected pleased her. Frederick might be too brutish to appreciate it, but she didn't care. If she expected the worst from him, then she couldn't be disappointed when that was what she got. Her problem had always been that she had expected his best in return for her best, and that's how she always ended up getting burned.

Doris scanned the dining room. She loved it. It was decorated perfectly. Of course, she had decorated it, but still no one could have done better. She closed her eyes and smelled the new fragrance on her wrist. *Ahh, yes.* Everything was perfect. Even an ignorant stone couldn't ignore all this. Doris prided herself on being the queen of perfection, and tonight she was on top of her game.

Doris gave her dining room one more glance and went back into her sparkling clean kitchen. She had worked all afternoon on the menu. Everything smelled divine. She had made a venison roast from a French cookbook. Frederick had shot the deer himself, so how could he not be pleased with that? And then a layered potato dish with expensive cheeses and cream. *Come on!* She could hardly wait herself. She had bought the freshest green beans and toasted almonds to sprinkle over the dish. Green beans were Frederick's favorite. Of course, there would be warm rolls and, another favorite, layered lemon chiffon and tender pastry for dessert.

They would start with a glass of sparkling Italian wine when he got home and spend a little time chatting about his day. He always loved to talk about himself, Lord knew. If he asked her about last night, she'd just say she had overreacted and apologize. Wouldn't he just love that if she actually apologized for something? She chuckled. Maybe she would try it just to see his reaction even if he didn't bring up last night. Yes. Yes, she would do it. As many things as she could do to throw him off their expected routine would be to her benefit.

She heard Frederick's truck door and started to hurry to greet him and then decided no, she would play this calm. She'd be detached, but alluring. She would offer hints, but no promises, stay close to him, but distant inside her heart. Expect nothing, and you can't be disappointed when you get nothing. So she would remain calm and expect a selfish slug to walk through the front door.

Frederick looked surprised when he came into the kitchen. Good. He had expected a difficult evening with her after last night, and instead, he had this. One for her.

He smiled tentatively. "Whatever it is smells great."

"Thank you," she said, coming around the counter with his chilled glass of prosecco.

Frederick took the glass. "I thought we were going out with the Edmonds tonight."

Doris frowned. Did they have other commitments? Maybe. She sipped her wine and tried to regain her edge. "I called and cancelled with them," she lied.

Frederick shrugged. "Okay, guess Bradley just hadn't got the word yet." Frederick sipped the wine and thought about it. "This is. . . new," he said.

"Yes, it is. I love it."

"Okay, then," Frederick said. "Guess I'll just go change if we are staying home."

"Oh, yes. Go get comfortable."

Frederick sat his glass down on the counter and headed for the stairs. Doris grabbed her cell phone and called Janice Edmonds. By the time Frederick came downstairs, Doris had resolved the problem and was back in the game.

"I've poured you some scotch. Do you want to relax and talk awhile, or are you ready for dinner?"

"Honestly, whatever you have cooking smells so good it would be hard to wait," Frederick said and sipped his scotch.

Oh, he was smooth, complimenting her food right away and wearing that new blue polo she liked that matched his eyes—matched his selfish old weasel eyes. Yes, that was better. "Fine," she said, finishing her prosecco and reaching for his prosecco glass still sitting on the counter where he'd left it. "Just go on in, and I'll have everything ready in no time."

Frederick went into the dining room and pulled out his chair. He sat down and took his phone out of his pocket. Doris watched as he sipped his scotch, read whatever, and waited like a king for his meal to be served. She had done a sorry job of training that man. Her next husband would insist that he stay and help her. Just look at all the work she must have done to make him such a fabulous meal—a meal superior to anything they could ever have gotten out in the finest restaurant, to be certain. Her next husband would find excuses to walk close behind her and brush up against her and then reach around her for a platter and touch her breast. They would shoot meaningful looks at each other, and she would feel contentment and love deep into her soul. Doris sighed. If she hadn't wanted to get Frederick set up for their impending painful divorce, then she would have chucked all the food in the trash and run upstairs and locked her door. But she was Doris, and she would see this through.

Doris fixed their two plates and carried them into the dining room. She sat the warm basket of rolls near Frederick and filled his water glass with frosty, cold water. She took her place at the other end of the table. Her next husband would insist that she sit next to him, where they could talk quietly and maybe hold hands while they were resting between courses.

Frederick clicked off his phone and picked up his fork and knife. He looked at the plate in front of him. "Did I forget our anniversary or something?"

Doris gasped. "After all these years, you don't even know . . ."

Frederick laughed at himself. "Of course, I know. I was just kidding. Is this venison?"

"I had to do something with it. You keep dragging those dreadful carcasses home."

"Well," he said, chewing a wad of meat, "guess I'll have to keep hunting if you can do this with the dreadful carcasses."

Doris relaxed a little. That was a compliment. She was getting him where she wanted him—fat and content and off guard. She went to sip the prosecco but found her glass was empty again. "Excuse me," she said, pushing her chair back. "I forgot to bring in the wine bottle."

"Sure," Frederick said, bending the long string bean to fit it in his mouth without cutting it.

Doris looked away. Her next husband would not only cut his green beans but also jump up to refill her wineglass. How had she lived like this for so long?

After dessert Frederick leaned back in his chair and looked at her. "Now what?"

Doris frowned. "What?"

"What do you want, Doris?"

Doris stood up—very serenely, she thought, despite the fury raging through her. Of course, she wanted something. She wanted him to appreciate her instead of suspect her of something devious. She wanted him to see her true value as a woman and a wife. She wanted him to realize how lucky he was before it was all snatched right out from under him. She just decided that she'd take the house in the divorce. He hadn't appreciated that either. Doris walked around the dining room and calmly blew out all the beautiful candles—little steady breaths, her back to him. She would not cave in. She wasn't just any mistreated old wife.

Frederick waited, but Doris just started clearing the table. He finally stood up and helped her carry the dishes back into the kitchen.

"Wouldn't it be easier if we just got this over with?" he finally asked.

Doris rinsed the plates without looking at him. "What does that mean?"

"Just talk about what is bothering you, and then we can get back to normal."

Doris looked up and smiled at him. She could do this. She had to do this. "I'm sorry, Frederick. I know I have been moody lately and, perhaps, have overreacted to things, so I made this lovely meal to try and make up for, well, for last night. I hope we can let it go now and just, as you put it, get back to normal."

Doris had been right. Her apology had him worried. He rubbed at the back of his neck and frowned at her.

"Seriously," Doris said, "go on. Isn't there some sport thingy on TV tonight? I've got this."

Frederick hesitated, and she knew she had won round one. He might go in the den and sit in front of the TV, but she knew he would be thinking about her. Doris flashed her dimply smile and flicked her hand at him to shoo him out of her kitchen.

Doris heard him refill his scotch glass and drop down into his leather chair. He waited a few minutes before he turned on the TV. Oh, she had him worried. Doris reached for the wine bottle but found it empty.

Walking past Elizabeth's door, her mother stopped dead still. She frowned and then turned her head to look into Elizabeth's room. First, her daughter's door was open. Elizabeth never left her door even ajar. Second, her window shade was up. There was actual daylight flooding the bedroom. And third was Elizabeth herself sitting in the center of her bed, legs crossed, apparently reading something, black hair tied back from her face. She wore a burgundy blouse and black jeans.

"Elizabeth?" her mother said cautiously.

Elizabeth lifted her head and smiled at her mother.

They looked at each other for a moment, and then Elizabeth's mother continued on her way downstairs.

Elizabeth uncurled her legs and stretched out straight on her bed. She sat the book on her abdomen and went back to reading. She had stopped by Daniel's shop after school to pick up the books he had offered and to ask him for a favor. She had felt a little awkward at first. Though she hadn't intentionally done anything wrong, her painting had awakened his sadness of reliving his wife's last moments. But no worries, Daniel had seemed very pleased to see her.

"Come in. I was hoping you would stop by," he'd said. "I have those books if you still want them."

"Yes, I do. Thank you," Elizabeth had said, walking slowly toward the counter. "And I was wondering if, because the show is only nine days away, if I could maybe come by after school and work on fixing my paintings? I mean I'd stay in the back out of the way if. . . if that would be okay."

"Sure. Of course. Do you want to start now?"

Elizabeth had nodded. "I don't want to show them the way they are. I mean, now that I know."

Daniel had smiled at her, so she'd felt brave enough to go on. "Now that I know about, you know, God."

Daniel had stood up and motioned her into the back room. "I was just looking at your painting this morning. It is amazing what a difference it made to just add the white. I would have suggested you mix colors in the white for different areas of the room, but your use of pure white . . . well, it works on its own. That's a talent, Twilight. Your vision is unique."

Elizabeth had stood studying her painting. "To be honest, it just came to me. I hadn't intended to add white. I thought I was finished with it. But it just seemed like what I had to do."

"Well, I can't wait to see what you do with the others you thought were finished."

Daniel had turned to go back into the front of the store while Twilight had set up her easel.

"If you don't mind," Twilight had said, stopping him, "do you think everyone could call me Elizabeth? My real name."

"Of course. Elizabeth is a beautiful name."

Elizabeth had shrugged. "Elizabeth never felt right, it was like just a word that I responded to but wasn't really me, and especially when I was going through my . . . my difficult time. I picked twilight because it felt dim, shadowy, you know, the kind of light that could be a little gloomy."

Daniel had thought about that. "You know, I see twilight as the soft, diffused light we get just before the sun dips below the horizon. It's a light that makes us pause and marvel at the beauty of the air."

Elizabeth had blushed then laughed. "You make me want to keep it."

"Well," Daniel had said, parting the curtain to go out into the shop, "whoever you are, you have talent and, I believe, a special wink from God."

Elizabeth had worked for two hours until it was time for Daniel to close his shop. If anyone had ever come into the store, she didn't know it. She was so inspired she couldn't see or hear anything but the thoughts in her head and the painting before her. How had she gone from invisible to being winked at by God?

"Dinner is ready," Elizabeth's mother called up the stairs.

Elizabeth stabbed her bookmark between the pages and closed Daniel's book. She jumped off the bed and bounded down the stairs. Her father was sitting at his place at the kitchen table, and her mother was setting a plate down in front of him. They stopped talking, and both glanced at each other, waiting to see what this new Elizabeth would do.

Elizabeth crossed to the sink and washed her hands. She opened the silverware drawer and picked out their forks and knives. "Yum, something really smells good," she said as she walked toward them.

"Pot roast and potatoes," her mother said. "But of course, I have a salad with cranberries and walnuts for you, Dear."

"Mom," she said, looking into her mother's worried face. "Dad," she said, looking into her father's worried face. "Twilight has left the building."

"What are you saying?" her mother asked, standing with the last plate still in her hands.

"Well, first, I will eat what you eat from now on. And I'm so sorry for all that ridiculous stuff I went through. I wish I could just rewind my life and do it over again. But in the last couple of days, I have learned things. God made me the way I am, and, well, who am I to be ashamed of God's work? It is not my job to change who I am, it's my job to just be the best me." She beamed at them.

"Oh no." Her mother wilted in front of Elizabeth's eyes. "I just can't."

Elizabeth frowned. "Can't what?"

"Dear, we love you," her father said as her mother began to tear up. "But now that we see where you are going, we have to talk about. . . well, about help. Therapy."

"Therapy? Therapy for what? Therapy for accepting who I am and deciding it's okay?"

"Elizabeth," her father went on, "your mother came down tonight and told me about you finally giving up that dark and scary phase you have put us all through. And we were hopeful. We want nothing more than for you to just be a normal teenager and enjoy this last year of high school. But. . ."

Elizabeth waited.

"But now with this God talk, it's obvious that you have gone way to the other end. We just want you in the middle and happy. That's all."

Elizabeth looked from one of them to the other. She had to give them the truth that her drawing away into her dark cocoon was not a pleasant experience for her parents. It hadn't been a fun place for her either—*just,* she thought, *a safer, less hurtful place at the time.* But now they were equating her discovering God as the far opposite of that? They felt believing in God was as radical as walking in a black cloud?

"God talk," Elizabeth repeated. "Are you saying you don't believe in God?"

Elizabeth's mother softened. "No, Dear, we are not saying that. We are just saying that we think you need help in figuring out, well, whatever it is that you are struggling with."

"I'm not struggling any longer. Now that I have ..." She wanted to say now that she had been winked at by God, but she knew that would really throw them into a tizzy. "I'm okay. Trust me. For the first time in a long time I feel good inside."

Her parents looked doubtful. "Would it hurt," her father asked, "if you, at least, talked to a therapist? We could go to one out of town if you'd be more comfortable."

Elizabeth shook her head. "What I want, what would make me feel better, is for you to give me some time. Granted, I have earned your confusion, but honestly, I think I have found what I need. Things have happened to me in the last couple of days that have changed me. I want to be happy about that and figure out where I need to go now. I don't need to feel like something is wrong with me any longer. I have felt that way long enough. I want to see light instead of darkness. And I believe accepting that God loves me just the way I am is a perfect place to start."

Her parents still looked doubtful. "It's your mother," Elizabeth's mother hissed and scowled at her husband.

"It's me," Elizabeth said. "It's just me. When you come to the art exhibit, you will see what happened to me. Now," she said, "that pot roast smells so good."

Eleanor sat in her swing on her back porch, reading the New Testament. It was a relief to see how much more she enjoyed reading this part of the Bible. She didn't want to have to abandon it because it had been too disturbing and confusing. She was certain that she would understand all that had troubled her about the Old Testament when she had finished with this part. Eleanor slowed her swing and picked up her cup of coffee to take a sip when she heard someone and glanced over the porch railing to see Fran stomping past.

"Good morning," Eleanor said

"Well, hello there," Fran called back as she continued on to the garden. "It might be a little late for the cucumbers, but the corn and hard squash look ready."

"Yes," Eleanor said, then added as though she needed to make the offer, "help yourself to whatever you like."

"Waste not, want not, I always say."

Eleanor went back to reading the parable of the prodigal son. She read it and reread it. It didn't make any sense that one son could be so selfish and thoughtless of the father's generosity that he could take his inheritance and squander it and then crawl back home while his brother had been faithful and conscientious and worked hard for his father, and then Jesus thought it was okay that the father rewarded the negligent son while telling his good and faithful son to accept his brother's return as a good thing.

Eleanor looked up from the Bible and frowned. There must be more to the story than this. What was she missing?

"You're going to have to get someone in here to till this all under pretty soon. Most of Bill's garden has gone by, and the weeds are taking over," Fran called from the garden.

"Yes, I will."

"I saw the Thompsons' son the other day. He is pretty lazy, but he's a big boy. I bet he could get this done in no time. Plus he probably wouldn't charge much. You being a widow and all." Fran straightened from her harvesting and stretched her aching back. "Always use that, Eleanor, people have a real soft spot for widows."

"I'll remember that, Fran."

Fran reached back down and pulled a fat radish from the earth. It had grown so large there was a huge split down the middle, and it looked corky from what she could see. What a waste. A neglected garden was a heartache—all that good food, and now look, just ruined from selfishness. Eleanor could have invited her over sooner before so much had gone to waste. Fran tossed the radish back into the dirt—all poor Bill's hard work wasted. Just wasted. And here his widow was more interested in painting and reading the Bible than tending to his garden. Some people.

Eleanor laid the satin ribbon on her page and closed the Bible. She stood up. "How is Milly? Have you heard from her since she left?"

Fran swatted at a fly that buzzed over her head. "Just that she got there. Not much else to tell. Those people are just like her. Like as not, they are just sitting around, fidgeting and fumbling in their own little world, totally oblivious to reality."

"When is she coming back?"

Fran frowned. "She didn't say exactly. I guess when they get sick of her and send her back. Should be pretty soon, I'd expect. That's why I have to make the most of this time. I'll get these vegetables cleaned and dried and ready for her to can when she gets back. Can't expect her to know how to do everything."

"Well, I hope she is having a good time with her family," Eleanor said, and Fran just harrumphed at that and went back to digging in the dirt.

Eleanor picked up her Bible and empty coffee cup. She paused, feeling like she should offer Fran something to drink, but not really wanting to entice her to stay longer than necessary. She was about to relent and call out to Fran when her phone rang. Fran picked her head up at the sound, and Eleanor just waved and escaped through the screen door.

"Hello," Eleanor said into the phone.

"Mom, I don't want any questions, I just want to know if I can come home. For a while, I mean. Until I get things figured out."

Oh dear, Eleanor thought. Her life was just beginning to get, well, comfortable. She was adapting and now Trish wanted to come home. Trish's return sort of felt like Fran moving in.

"Of course. Of course. You don't even have to ask."

"Okay, and, Mom, can you send me money for the trip? To rent a truck and for gas."

"You're moving all your stuff back?"

"Yes, I don't want to pay for storage here when I may decide to move somewhere else. I mean, coming back north just before winter isn't going to be pleasant, but there are warmer places I can move to later when I'm back on my feet, places that have more opportunities."

"How much do you need?"

"Probably five hundred dollars. I will, of course, pay you back when I get a job."

"When are you coming?"

"As soon as I get the money. And is it okay if I bring someone? It's only temporary like I said."

Eleanor sighed and closed her eyes. Anxiety tightened her chest. She tried not to remember how much Trish had put them through before she had left home. She tried not to remember the guilt she had felt that she was, on some level of unmotherliness, relieved to see Trish drive away. She had hoped, at that time, that maybe she and Bill could just get a rest, and then Trish would return one day all grown up and . . . easier to love.

Eleanor wrote down where to wire the money and promised Trish that she would go right now to her bank and then to the closest Western Union site to send it to her in Florida. Already she could feel her heart race. It's only temporary. It's only temporary.

Eleanor stuck her head out the back door to let Fran know that she had to run out. She didn't know why she had to report to Fran, but it didn't seem right to leave her there in the garden, thinking that Eleanor was in the house. Eleanor went to the front door and took her purse from the coat closet. She hoped that man Trish was with at Bill's funeral wasn't the someone Trish was bringing. He was, well, not the sort Eleanor would pick for her daughter to be involved with. Maybe today, when she got home from her errand, she would open that bottle of red wine she had in the pantry.

⌇⌇⌇

Doris sat at the kitchen table, staring out at her flower garden in the backyard. She sipped her tepid coffee and put the rose-painted cup back into its saucer. It was almost ten o'clock and she was still sitting in her bathrobe, drinking coffee. She hadn't showered or done her hair and makeup. She was falling into ruin because of Frederick. His disinterest was just draining the life out of her. No one was more positive, more energetic and fun than Doris. No one could bring a room to life like Doris. No one could have given more to a man than she had. And now she was empty. He had drained the life out of her.

Doris sighed loudly into the quiet kitchen. What to do? What to do? Doris looked at her fingernails. They still looked pretty good. She could go to the nail salon today before her appointment with the attorney, but tomorrow was her regularly scheduled appointment at the nail salon, so she might as well wait. She looked out into the backyard. She could, maybe, get on her sun hat and garden gloves and work in the flowerbeds for an hour or two. She knew they needed weeding and thinning but to be honest, she just didn't have the heart for it today. Nothing felt worth it. What was the point? This was the day she was starting divorce proceeding against Frederick, and that knowledge alone had soured everything else. She wished, for the first time, that she wasn't so important, such a prominent figure in town. If she were just any other marginal housewife, then she would probably have another marginal housewife as a friend to confide in, and she would be sitting in someone else's kitchen right now, sobbing and hiccupping and going on and on about how wretched Frederick was, how cold and distant and unappreciative, and how no matter how hard she tried, he just took her for granted. But because she was who she was, she couldn't trust anyone else with her personal business. She had to keep up appearances no matter the cost.

Doris slid her chair back and stood up. Enough. She had to get a grip. She would go upstairs and pick out her most flattering suit, the coral one that was tailored at the waist. She wanted the attorney to begin their relationship with questioning what kind of man could push such an amazing woman to such depths of misery that she would have to leave him. Once she had taken this courageous first step in her battle against Frederick, she was certain that she would be her old self again. It was the helpless way that Frederick made her feel that was the most difficult to bear. It was like, after all these years, he still had the power to control her happiness.

Doris crossed the kitchen and caught a glimpse of a figure getting out of a truck in front of her house. She scowled and stuck her face out farther to see better. Yes, some furniture truck was in front of her house, and a man was coming up her front steps. Doris panicked; she couldn't open the door at ten in the morning, looking like this. What could she do? What could she do?

The man knocked on the door, and Doris pulled herself together and calmly walked over and opened the door a crack. The man identified himself and said he was there to make a delivery. Doris assured him, through the crack in the door, that she had not ordered anything, so he must be at the wrong house. The man read the address on his delivery slip, and it was her address.

"Well, I'm sorry, but I haven't ordered anything to be delivered from your company. Please go away."

The man stood there a moment just looking at her eye peering out at him. "I have a card. You can call my company if you are worried this isn't legitimate," he said.

"I'm not accusing you of being illegitimate, I'm just saying that I know I haven't ordered anything from your company."

The man nodded and turned to leave. He glanced back once on his way to his truck, and she quickly closed the door. She could see the man making a phone call, and she felt better. He would get his facts straight and go away. She had better make herself presentable. Obviously, one could never tell when one would be surprised by an unwelcome visitor. Doris was heading toward the stairs when the housephone rang. She hesitated then went to answer it.

"Hello."

"Doris, is there a delivery man at the house right now?" Frederick asked, his voice a bit huffy.

"Well, yes. There is, but I can assure you that I have not ordered anything to be delivered." Doris smiled a little. Apparently, Frederick was spying on her. He even knew when a misrouted delivery truck was at their house.

"Well, let them in, for god's sake. I ordered this. I just told the guy to give me a few minutes to talk to you and then to bring the delivery in."

"Delivery? What is it?"

"You'll see. Just open the door, and let them bring it in."

"Okay," Doris said and hung up the phone. This was so unusual. Frederick never picked out anything for the house, not even for his own office. She had spent days getting it just right, and then he had barely noticed the details. He had walked into the room when she had presented it and nodded. He liked it, he had said. She had to then literally walk him through each detail so that he would see how perfect it actually was. And now he had picked some random something or other out without even consulting her?

Doris was so unsettled that she opened the door for the deliveryman while she was still in her bathrobe and had no makeup on.

"This goes in the master bedroom," the deliveryman said, waiting for Doris to direct him.

Doris led the way upstairs. Whatever it was, it was long and had wrapping taped around it.

"Okay, where do you want it?"

Doris looked around the room. Something would have to be moved to fit such a thing as this unless... it stood upright because it was a gun cabinet. No, he wouldn't dare!

"Unwrap it so I can see where to put it," Doris instructed the men.

"Oh!" Doris said, stepping back when the wrapping was removed. "Oh my." Doris stood with her hand on her mouth, just staring at what Frederick had done. He had bought the very chaise lounge that she had shown him a picture of in a magazine. He had glanced at it and mumbled that it was nice, but never, never in her life had he actually purchased something like this that she had seen in a magazine. It was beautiful—white and soft. She had to walk over and run her hand over the fabric. She was right; the wood grain on the frame and the legs perfectly matched her bedroom furniture. It was just as fabulous as she had expected.

"Where would you like us to put it?" the deliveryman asked again.

Doris stepped back and surveyed her room. Of course, it should go there opposite the window. She had pictured herself lounging there with, perhaps, a glass of rosé and a book and glancing up now and again to catch that pink glow of a perfect summer sunset flooding into her bedroom.

"Do you mind signing this delivery slip?"

"What? Oh yes. Yes, of course," Doris said, taking the clipboard. She scribbled her name and handed it back, still not believing how perfectly it had fit in her room.

"Okay, we will just take all this wrapping mess and let ourselves out, then."

Doris nodded and walked over to sit on the lounge. Oh yes, this was perfect. As soon as the men left her room, she lifted her legs and stretched out on the lounge. She sighed. This was her. This was so perfectly her. She knew she had to have it as soon as she'd seen the picture. And to think their very own little local furniture store had actually had it in stock. Doris relaxed and wished she knew how to take a selfie with her cell phone because she would do it and send it to . . . whom? No one came to mind. Well, anyway, she knew she looked wonderful on it.

Doris heard the front door close and the truck drive off. She stroked the white fabric and smiled until a horrid thought jumped out and ruined her contentment. Frederick had sent this. She had an appointment with an attorney to divorce Frederick in just three hours, and now he had done *this*. It was so like him to never spontaneously give her anything this wonderful until the very day she was going to start divorce proceedings against him. How could he have guessed what she was planning and then thought of this to throw her off? Wait. Of course, he was probably having her phone calls monitored, so then surely, he would have known about her calling to make the appointment.

Doris sat up. This was terrible news. The divorce papers were supposed to be a surprise. Frederick was supposed to be sitting in his office at work, feeling all bossy and confident, and then, bam, right out of the blue he would be interrupted from his self-importance and handed the devastating news that he was losing the most loving and most wonderful wife in the world. That was how it was supposed to be.

Doris stood up and paced around the room. Everything was ruined. Frederick knew. He had followed her and spied on her, and now he had even traced her phone calls. Doris paused at the new chaise lounge and mournfully stroked its soft fabric. The most wonderful gift was now ruined because Frederick had sent it just to make her feel guilty about divorcing him. He probably thought her resolve would crumble when she finally got one thoughtful gift from him that she hadn't actually picked out and purchased herself. Oh, she could see him right now, grinning like a smug fool at his desk, imagining her so overcome with joy and gratitude that she would forget all the suffering she had endured that had pushed her to divorce him. Well, he once again had underestimated her. She was keeping that appointment, and she was definitely getting the chaise lounge in the divorce settlement.

Pauline added the last brushstroke to the second canvas. She had known when she had finished the first that there was going to be three. The first was the one where there was more burgundy than blue. The second canvas she had painted with more blue than burgundy, but with the same type of white-and-gray swirls. And the third canvas, which would actually be in the center of the three, would be equal amounts of burgundy and blue, and the swirls would be only white. It was exciting for her to paint a trilogy. Maybe the paintings wouldn't make sense to anyone else, maybe no one else would catch the obvious differences, but it worked for her—just enough different to be their own piece, but definitely enough alike to make a complete whole. Pauline had no idea where this inspiration had come from. She had never seen anything like this. But it certainly made her heart swell with pride.

There, she thought, cleaning her brushes; she might have time to bring the first canvas to Daniel's shop before the kids got home from school. The first one was dry and transportable, and she could explain the other two. Of course, Daniel didn't even know she was painting at home as well as on Tuesday nights. A flutter of apprehension gripped her at the sudden thought that maybe Daniel wouldn't get what she was trying to do. He would, as always, be gentle, reassuring, and encouraging with her, but for some reason, it was important to her that he react with enthusiasm when he contemplated her vision. Perhaps she would wait until the third canvas was completed, and then he would surely understand.

Pauline cleaned all her tools and paint tubes and closed them up in their box. She carried everything back into the attic so they would be safe from the kids' rambunctiousness and Tim's questioning eyes. She felt like a spy or a thief, like she was leading a dual secret life. She had decided, after disrupting everyone's life yesterday, to never work on her paintings when her family was home. She would never even talk about her art to them. Oh, they knew she was painting and would notice that something about her had changed. They might even feel a little resentful of this new piece of her life that didn't include them; that wasn't about them or even for them, but she couldn't stop. She couldn't go back to the way she was. She wasn't certain at times what she would do if she had to choose. The thought troubled her even though she knew it would never be like that. Tim would never make her give it up. The kids would adapt. She just had to find a balance, was all.

Pauline came down from the attic and pushed the ladder steps back up, protecting her secret life. She then turned and faced the house. Oh my, this couldn't be her house. Pauline glanced at the clock. She had forty-five minutes to get everything done. She rushed to make the kids' beds and gather their dirty clothes. She closed the door to her and Tim's room—no time for that—and then moved on to the kitchen. Good grief! Had she done nothing today except close the door behind the kids and scurry to the attic for her paints?

Pauline scraped and rinsed the breakfast dishes and loaded them into the dishwasher. She cleared the counter and actually felt the physical guilt of throwing away the package of sandwich meat because she had forgotten to put it in the refrigerator after making their lunches. She grabbed a handful of Cheerios and stuffed them in her mouth as she closed up the box. She hadn't even eaten lunch. She hadn't even, she realized now, finished her second cup of coffee that sat cold on the counter.

Pauline sank down in a chair at the table. She would have to admit that there was something terribly wrong with her. She tried to keep up, but her life was out of control. She was disappointing everyone who depended on her. She didn't have a grip on the house or her kids, and she hadn't visited her mother at the nursing home for several weeks—inexcusable! Tim was picking up more of her chores after he had worked a long day. Even she herself was being neglected. It wasn't just because she was painting. There was something else that had changed. She was tired. She wasn't organized. She . . . was losing interest in all that had filled her before. A tear broke out and raced down her cheek.

The phone rang and Pauline thought of not answering it. But of course, she could never be that rude, and besides, it could always be some terrible news about one of the kids or Tim. She jumped from her chair and grabbed up the phone.

"Hello, Dear," her mother said.

"Oh, Mom, I'm so sorry I haven't been by, but. . ."

"Don't worry. I'm fine. I just wanted to check in and see how you all were. Tim and the kids. And you, of course."

"Everyone is fine."

"Good. Good."

"Mom, I have started painting. Like painting paintings, I mean. You know, like art paintings."

Her mother chuckled. "That does not surprise me. You were always talented."

"I was?"

"Yes, why do you sound like that? You were always more interested in art than Philip and Patricia."

Pauline frowned. She remembered her sister as more artistic than herself. Patricia could copy anything, and you could hardly notice the difference. Patricia always colored better than Pauline. In fact, Patricia was always the one everyone came to for help with their school projects and posters. "Mom, you must mean Patricia."

"No, dear, I know my own children. Patricia always did more with her art, but you were more interested in the details of art. I could see you were afraid to compete with her, but the way you saw things was much more artistic than your sister. Art isn't just about copying, though Patricia was good, it is about having an eye that sees the world differently than the average person. I remember how you would drag me outside every time there was a rainbow or sunset, and we would just stand there on the stoop and watch the colors change. You kids always collected fall leaves and pressed them between wax paper, and your arrangement was always more colorful, more thoughtful, and more artfully arranged. Why, for years I kept those little counting books you made with pictures of brightly colored balls and cubes and triangles."

"I don't remember any of that."

"Oh, that's because it was just you being you. But trust me, they were special. I wish I still had them. There is so much I wish I could go back and get."

There was a long silence on the phone as Pauline's mother was remembering her lost treasures and as Pauline was trying to remember if she ever thought she was artistic. She knew that she had wanted to be like her sister. But she had always accepted that she never could be. That was probably why she had gotten the paints in her attic to begin with—to test herself in the safety and privacy of her own home. But she had failed and hidden her paintings away. Until now. Now Daniel had redirected her vision, and she felt hopeful— hopeful, but frightened. It would be almost too much to bear if everyone at the art show ignored her paintings for the real ones.

"Well," her mother said, "I will let you go. I just wanted to check on you. Maybe you can bring one of your paintings for my room."

"I'd love to, Mom, but I'm afraid I have reverted back to my counting-book phase."

"Well, wouldn't I just love that?"

<hr>

Elizabeth felt a little awkward when she first approached the school. How does one go from pretending to be normal to then pretending to being invisible to now wanting to be normal again? Her heart was in this, but old insecurities were stubborn things. She felt the other students noticing her, but knowing she wasn't alone anymore, she looked right at them instead of down. She smiled, and they smiled a confused flicker of a smile back at her, then they looked away as though they were not supposed to notice that her hair had been dyed back to its soft brown color and that her clothes were real—like real blue jeans and a simple pink T-shirt. Even her black book bag had been replaced with a denim one. Some of them even stole a second glance and frowned, but she didn't care. Today she was determined to be who she was, and that made her happy.

Elizabeth's parents were still worried that she was just going through another difficult stage, but what could they do when she continued on for the rest of her life believing in God and herself? Eventually, they would have to believe and accept that she was now and forever who she was made to be. Elizabeth carried her mother's Bible in her book bag and intended to read it at lunch. Why not? She loved to read—always had. Why was this so different? Knowledge was knowledge, and she wanted to know. She wanted to read the stories Gram had told her. She wanted to believe, so she would move forward with her reading and her painting and her new confidence until it all just clicked into place.

Elizabeth slipped into her desk in her first-period class. She took out her notebook and pen and sat up straight. She felt, for some reason, that she was really going to enjoy Ms. Harmon's lecture in humanities class. She sat waiting for class to start, anticipating a good day, when a note was passed to her from the side. She felt a bump on her arm and looked over to see one of the other dark children whom she had talked to—not ever as a friend, actually, just someone close enough to her strangeness to associate with when necessary. Franklin jabbed the folded-up paper so she would see the urgency of taking it before the teacher noticed.

Elizabeth took the note and opened it. "What is with you?" was all that was written on the note. Elizabeth smiled and wrote on the back of his paper, "God loves you!" and passed it back.

Franklin read the note and pulled his head back. Whoa, this was unexpected. Elizabeth knew that word would spread among the dark circle before the day was through. She felt light inside and started earnestly taking notes as the teacher spoke.

At lunch Elizabeth selected a table on the side of the room, as she usually did, and took out her usual bag of sliced green peppers and another bag of fruit-and-nut granola to go with her bottled carrot juice. Then she did something totally unusual—she took out a Bible and opened it. She had eaten the same food, sat in the same place, and read a book for years, and no one had really noticed. But today, because she was someone confusing, someone even stranger than she had been, people noticed.

Pamela, also known as Panda in some circles, came and sat down opposite Elizabeth. "What are you reading?"

Elizabeth lifted the edge of the book so Panda could see. "I can't believe I have never read this before," Elizabeth said. "Of all the books I have read in my life, I have neglected to read the most famous book ever written." She shrugged and laughed. "How is that?"

"Because," Panda said, flipping her black-and-white hair out of her eyes, "the Bible is not supposed to be brought to school."

"Really? How do you know that?" Elizabeth asked.

"Well, everyone knows that. Duh, the separation of church and state."

"I have sat at this table and read books on witchcraft and demons and goblins, and no one objected. Some people actually believe in that stuff. I mean cults and demon worshipping are okay with the state, but not the Bible? Seriously?"

Panda looked confused. "All I know is that you are not supposed to have a Bible on school property. At least that is what I believe the rules are."

Elizabeth nodded. "I probably would have thought that too before I . . . well, whatever, now I know I would have been wrong. Not only is it okay to bring it and read it, but also it is what I wish I had been reading all along."

"What happened to you?" Panda asked.

"God winked at me," Elizabeth said and then watched Panda's eyes widen with disbelief.

"Really," Elizabeth said, "I believe that."

Panda got up and glanced back at Elizabeth one more time before she joined her table of dark souls.

Bring it, Elizabeth thought as they leaned in to hear the disturbing news. Though Elizabeth was never really one of them, she was close enough that they were confused, and in all seriousness, they felt a bit betrayed by her sudden abandonment of her darkness.

"Can we sit with you?"

Elizabeth looked up at Brandon and Cathy. They were not in the elite clique, but pretty near. Let's just say they did not have to envy any group as they were so obviously well liked and content in their skin.

Elizabeth nodded, and they sat down opposite her.

"Word has it," Cathy said, "that you are moving out into the light."

Elizabeth frowned, not certain where they were going.

"We just wanted you to know that we belong to a Christian youth group and would like to invite you to join us. We meet on Wednesdays after school."

"Thanks," Elizabeth said, "but I don't really know all that much yet. I mean I just started to . . . believe."

Brandon smiled. "We all had to start somewhere. You don't have to be a biblical scholar. You just have to want to be a follower of Jesus."

Now it was Elizabeth's turn to pull back. Being happy with her new inner faith was one thing, but coming out and admitting to being a follower of Jesus… it just felt awkward somehow, too bold a move when she hadn't even gotten to know Jesus as Jesus. She sort of lumped Him in with God, so of course, she believed in Him, but she wasn't sure who He was to proclaim herself as an actual follower of His. He would know if she was superficial, and that couldn't be good.

"No pressure," Cathy said. "We just wanted you to know that you are welcome whenever you are ready."

"Thanks," Elizabeth said and smiled weakly as they got up and walked away together. Her heart was pounding, and she was certain her face was flushed. This moving into the light was more complicated than she had expected. Alone in her room or with her fellow artists, she was confident of what was happening to her. But when faced with her peers who actively followed Jesus, she felt terribly inferior. And then add to that an actual invitation to belong to their group. She would never have dreamed that would happen to her.

Elizabeth closed her Bible and gathered up her lunch debris. She needed to get to her next class before someone else approached her.

Ruthie adjusted the plunging neckline of her waitress top. She could wear pretty much what she wanted at the Bar & Grill as long as the top was white and the bottom was black, so she chose a top that could show a lot or be adjusted to hide most of her breasts— depending if she was serving a table of guys or a family. Tonight was mostly men, so she tugged the neckline a little lower. It was a sorted business, but it paid the bills.

"What will it be, boys?" she said, appearing at their round table.

"Tonight we are celebrating, Ruthie," one of the men said. "Eddie got that promotion he was hoping for, so it will be double shots of your best whiskey to begin with. And, oh yeah, put it on Eddie's tab." Everyone at the table laughed at that, and Eddie looked a little worried and then shrugged.

"Actually," the man said, "I'll have a Bud." Eddie looked relieved.

Ruthie got all the orders and then went to the bar. Max was sitting there as usual. He was drinking a beer and eating a hamburger. Max had come straight from the gravel pit so he was not at his best. His hair had been combed and his hands were clean, so Ruthie gave him a pass.

"How's work?" she asked Max, hoping he'd grumble and threaten to leave as he usually did.

Max shrugged. "It's work. How is it supposed to be?"

"Well, there have been times when you had a definite opinion about your day. Just checking, is all."

Ruthie handed her bar request to the bar tender and decided to pick at Max's blasé attitude a little more. "Heard someone got fired today. Thought maybe it was you."

"No one got fired."

"Guess I can't trust anything I hear," she said. "But if you had been fired, where do you think you would go?"

Max put his hamburger down and scowled at her. "Woman, what are you babbling about?"

"Just wondering if you had, you know, a place you'd like to move to if you got fired or quit your job."

"Nope," he said and went back to his hamburger.

Ruthie waited for her bar order. She would miss Max. He was always in a foul mood, which she liked, but he had a good heart. She hoped he'd find someone when she was gone who could see the good underneath the foul.

Ruthie was just setting the beers on the table, bending a little lower over the table than probably necessary to accomplish the task, when the door opened and a family of four came in. They waited by the door to be seated, the dad apparently surveying the place to determine if he wanted his family to eat there. Ruthie sat the drink tray on the empty table behind her and went over to greet and seat them.

Upon closer inspection, she could see they were a little ragged—clean enough, but their clothes and shoes had seen better days. Ruthie always noticed these things as one who depended on the generosity of her customers for her paycheck. This family would definitely not be able to spare the extra for a good tip. Normally, she would have seated them, done the minimum of service requirements, and be glad to see them on their way. But tonight, maybe because the two teenage girls tugged at her heart or maybe because she still had the shadow of God watching her every move, Ruthie seated them with politeness and patience. She promptly got them menus, and then, she didn't know why, she rattled off a list of amazing specials that were not on the menu. She even made up amazing prices. What?

The family asked for a few minutes to talk, and Ruthie left them. She was supposed to go to the table of beer drinkers and get their food orders, but instead she went to the beverage station and filled four large glasses with soda and carried them back to the family.

"Of course, you can order any other drinks you like, all beverages are free tonight," she said. "But I thought I'd just start you with these. They are very cold. We have coffee and tea if you'd rather."

The family looked surprised. "Free? Really?" the mother asked.

Ruthie nodded. "Yup."

"This is fine, thank you," the father said.

Ruthie nodded twice again. "Good, I'll just go see to another table and be right back."

She took the men's orders and refilled other customers' drinks then returned to the family. "What will it be?"

They asked her the price of a couple of specials, and she couldn't remember exactly what she had told them, so she said that she would have to double-check with the cook, but she was pretty sure they were the super-duper special tonight and so very cheap. "You know how it is," she said, "the cook orders too much of something, and then we have to push it to get rid of it."

The father nodded and said they would all like the roast-beef plate.

"Coming right up," Ruthie said. "Be right back with salad and bread."

The family all looked at one another. Something didn't feel right. "That is included in the price?" the father asked.

"Oh yeah. And dessert is included. I hate to brag, but we do make the best pies here."

Ruthie left them looking a little bewildered at their good fortune and brought their order to the cook.

"Hey, Manny, could you be a little generous on these plates? I have really hungry people out here."

Manny shrugged. "All my meals are generous."

"Thanks."

Ruthie collected the plates to serve another table and stole glances at the family as she went past. This family did tug at her heart, especially the girls. She hoped her girls sat as straight and were as soft-spoken as these girls. Then she laughed out loud—right, soft-spoken; they were still her daughters whether she had raised them or not. God only knew what kind of trouble they were causing their father.

Ruthie brought their parade of super-duper cheap food to their table and then concentrated her waitressing skills on the table of men. Her regulars were always good-enough tippers, but she would need to do better tonight if she was going to cover the cost of the four drinks, dinners, and desserts.

When the family had finally left with their to-go boxes of pie and leftover dinner rolls, she stood with her hands on her hips and smiled. She felt good—really good as though she had been given something instead of doing the giving. They had tried to protest, but she told them a mystery diner had paid their tab and had left the building, so there was no haggling to be done about it. "Even the tip?" the father had asked. Ruthie had assured him that even the tip was paid, and it was very generous, so she actually owed them a thank-you for coming in.

Max had sat close enough to hear Ruthie's performance. If that woman wasn't careful, he might have to ask her to marry him.

Eleanor shook out the bottom sheet and stretched it over the mattress in the guest room. Knowing Trish, her guest would probably not be using this room, but on the slight chance they might care about appearances, Eleanor should freshen it. Eleanor continued making the bed and then pulled her mother's hand-crocheted doilies off the dresser and the nightstand. They would need to be hand washed. She opened the window just a couple of inches to let a cool breeze sweep through the room.

"Oh, Bill," she said and then sighed. "What am I getting myself into?" Eleanor hadn't heard from Trish since she had sent the money, so all Eleanor could surmise was that the

U-Haul was probably loaded and on its way. Trish and her friend should be here by Saturday evening. How much stuff was Trish bringing? Where would they store it all? Would they just sit around and let Eleanor cook and clean for them? They obviously didn't have any money, or they wouldn't have had to borrow—ask—for money from her. How long would it take them to get on their own and move somewhere else far away?

Eleanor left the guest room and glanced into Trish's room. It still looked like the room of a teenager, and for all Eleanor knew, her daughter had not grown beyond that. Here she was in her mid thirties and she had nothing but a few pieces of furniture to show for her life's work. Eleanor had noticed a pixie or fairy tattoo on Trish's ankle when she had come home for her father's funeral. Trish had three earrings in each ear and one silver ball pierced through one of her eyebrows. What was the sense in that?

Eleanor walked into the room and sat on the foot of the bed. She had to admit that there had been wonderful moments when Trish was little—those sweet ponytails bouncing as she ran with her baby-doll arms spread to meet her father when he had come home from work. That image could still bring tears to her eyes. And then Trish would snuggle in Eleanor's lap and twiddle her hair as her mother read her favorite stories. And then she stood on her red wooden step stool to help her mother make cookies—peanut butter cookies. Trish would concentrate, her little eyebrows puckered, as she poked a Hershey kiss into the exact center of each soft ball of dough. Maybe Eleanor would make some peanut butter cookies and surprise Trish.

Eleanor felt a little better from the memories. She stood up to leave Trish's room and go assess her pantry staples when someone knocked on her front door. Eleanor hurried down the stairs and into the front room. She could see Fran's outline through the curtain in the door. Her heart sank. What now? The garden was pretty well gone by.

Fran was standing on the porch, a jar of pickles in her hand. Against her better judgment, Eleanor invited her in. Fran stepped into the room and held out the jar of pickles.

"These are last year's batch, so you'd better get to them soon. I have a fresh batch brining, but it'll be a few days before I can do anything with them."

Eleanor took the pickles. "You really didn't need to bring me anything. As you said, I wouldn't have been able to use all that the garden produced anyway."

"Oh, I know. I know that, but a good neighbor doesn't take without repaying."

"Well, thank you again," Eleanor said as they both just stood there and looked at each other. Finally, it was obvious that Fran did not intend to deliver the pickles and leave, so Eleanor asked if she would like a cup of tea maybe.

"That sounds good. It'll warm me up. It's definitely fall out there. I'm not happy about that. Fall means winter is just around the corner."

"Yes, that is true," Eleanor said, leading Fran into the kitchen and filling the teakettle with water.

"Speaking of colder weather, I see you opened your front windows upstairs. You airing out the house for company?"

Eleanor turned the burner on under the teakettle and took a moment to answer Fran. Was there a point in not telling Fran when soon enough she would see the U-Haul? At least if Fran knew ahead of time, she wouldn't have to be over here the moment Trish got home, poking her nose in everything. "You are very astute," Eleanor said. "Would you like anything in your tea? Milk? Sugar? Honey?"

"Honey if it is local. If all you've got is that store-bought in that little bear, then no thanks."

"It's local," Eleanor said then decided to stall as long as she could. She knew Fran would not leave without an answer, but Eleanor somehow felt better if Fran had to work for it. "Have you heard from Milly? When will she be coming back?"

Fran sat down at the table and glanced around the kitchen. When was the last time Eleanor changed her wallpaper? The seam was curling a little there just above the stove. How did she not see that? A stepladder and a little paste were all it would take. If she didn't want to bring her wallpaper into the current century, she could at least make it more presentable. Certainly, Eleanor had enough money to hire a handyman to do it for her. There was just no excuse for letting the place go.

"When is Milly coming back?" Eleanor repeated.

"Oh, who knows? I haven't heard a word from her since she got there. And that is fine with me. That woman can get on your last nerve."

"So you are enjoying your time alone?"

"Oh yes. Yes. I have everything I need. Though," Fran said and chuckled at herself, "I do have some projects for her when she gets back. Milly was always easier to live with if you kept her busy."

Eleanor put the tea bags on the edge of the saucers and sat down at the table to wait for the water to boil.

"So who's coming?" Fran asked.

"Trish is coming on Saturday."

Fran slapped the table. "Good. I'm glad I got through to that girl."

"You? What did you do?"

"Well, I'm sorry to say, but someone had to step in and wake up that girl's conscience. She and her man friend, whatever his name was, left right after the funeral, and she never looked back. We are all accountable for one another. That's why I had to take Milly in after her husband died. I knew it wouldn't be easy, but family is family."

"Well," Eleanor said, "thank you for looking out for me."

"How long is she staying?"

"She didn't say."

"Is she bringing that man, what's his name, back with her? He looked a little shifty. A little too dark skinned to be an American."

Eleanor signed. Did Fran ever listen to herself? "I understand a lot of people in Florida have tans. The sun shines there a lot."

"True. True. But there was something foreign about him. Like it wasn't a natural tan."

"I'm afraid I don't remember what shade his tan was."

"Oh, of course, not! You were burying your husband. It wasn't expected that you would be aware of everything at a time like that."

The water came to a boil and Eleanor gratefully stood up to retrieve the teakettle.

"So, is he coming too?" Fran persisted.

"I don't know. I didn't ask."

"Well, she is probably coming home because they broke up. I saw that Trish had put on some weight when she was home. She was always so thin. I used to worry about her health when she was little. So frail and all skinny arms and legs. But at the funeral she was quite a few pounds overweight, if you asked me. Of course, she is getting up there in age, so that's when the pounds just start adding on. Can't be helped, believe me. But everyone knows those foreign-type men only like the shapely young girls."

Eleanor waited for Fran to put her tea bag in the cup, and then she poured the boiling water over it. "You may be right," Eleanor said, pouring her own water. What was the sense of ever trying to reason with Fran?

"Of course, I'm right. I watch enough TV to know that."

"Tell me," Eleanor said, sitting down opposite Fran. "Do you understand the parable of the prodigal son in the Bible?"

Fran frowned. "I'm certain I could, but I'd have to read it again to remember. Some of us don't have the luxury to just sit around and read."

"I appreciate that," Eleanor said, wanting to add that it must be straining to run one's own house while at the same time trying to stick your nose into everyone else's. But of course, she could never bring herself to say such a thing. She wondered now, with talking about the Bible, if thinking ugly things was equally as wicked as saying them.

"I saw the posters for the art show next week," Fran said to change the subject. "How many paintings are you putting in?"

"I have three I think will be ready."

"What are they? What do you paint?"

Eleanor shrugged. "It seems I like road pictures."

"Road pictures?"

"Well, country roads. You know, with trees overhanging the road and maybe rough wooden fencing with wildflowers and vines."

"Well, I don't want to burst your bubble, but they don't sound all that interesting. Do they have people in them?"

"No. I am definitely not talented enough for people."

"Well, you should think of adding some before the show. If you are not good at faces, then paint them from the back. Anyone can paint the back of a head."

"I'll think about it," Eleanor said as Fran loudly sipped at her hot tea. Eleanor smiled to herself; certainly, having Trish back couldn't be as difficult as this.

Doris was waiting for Frederick to get home from work. She was in the living room with a glass of wine already poured for herself and a scotch for Frederick. Frederick liked his scotch over ice, but he did not like it too watery, so she had to wait until she heard his truck before she added the ice. She was a bit unnerved from her meeting with her attorney. Oh, she was going through with the divorce even though the attorney had listened to her list of grievances and suggested they try marriage counseling first. Marriage counseling? Frederick would never discuss his faults with anyone, especially a stranger, no matter the marriage counselor or the list of certificates framed on his wall. No, counseling was out, which, she pointed out to the attorney, was just another example of how difficult her husband was.

Doris had worked herself into a state on the drive to the attorney's office. She had always prided herself on never letting details ruffle her, but today Frederick had pulled another sneaky move by having the chaise lounge delivered just when she was practically out the door. Okay, she had lounged around for as long as she could before getting ready for her appointment, she definitely loved the chaise lounge, but she did not appreciate the timing. How could Frederick always know how to get to her?

On the drive over, she had made a couple of unnecessary turns in case Frederick was having her followed, but thankfully, when she got to the attorney's office, she did not detect any suspicious cars in the area.

Doris sipped her wine. She had decided to thank Frederick for the gift and then go about their usual routine. Oh, he knew what was going on, but he wouldn't get the satisfaction of forcing her to admit it. He would just have to wait for her to make her move on her own time. She had told the attorney not to serve Frederick the papers until after the art show. She was putting her energies and money into making that event one for the town to talk about for years to come. Then Frederick would be served, and everyone would pity him for losing such an amazing woman. So let Frederick throw diversions at her, she would have the last word, and he would be sorry.

Ahh, there was the weasel now. Doris took a large slug of wine and readied herself. She was not to be trifled with when she had a mission.

Frederick came into the foyer and dropped his briefcase on the mahogany table as though she had not told him repeatedly not to do that. He had an office, and it belonged there, not in the entry where it was in everyone's face when they walked in the door. She supposed the attorney wouldn't think that was important either. Well, unfortunately, her attorney was a man; she could only expect so much understanding from another self-centered man.

Frederick smiled when he saw her waiting there with their drinks. Doris contained her distain.

"How was your day?" Frederick asked, coming into the room.

"Well," she said, playing his game, "I had a lovely surprise today. Thank you so much. But I truly don't know what I did to deserve it."

"No reason, really. I just knew you would like it," Frederick said, coming toward her.

Doris hoped he didn't expect a kiss for doing something thoughtful for a change. But Frederick just picked up his glass and fished a couple of cubes out of the ice bucket. Doris cringed. Was he blind or just that crude, using his, most likely, unwashed hands to pick up the ice cubes rather than using the tongs hanging on the side of the ice bucket? Oh yes, the attorney thought her life was easy just because Frederick didn't beat her and paid the bills!

Frederick eased himself down into the chair opposite her and sipped at his scotch. "So did you lounge around all day on it?"

Doris bristled. "Of course, not. I had things to do. Appointments to keep."

Frederick nodded. "I see. Well, I hope you get to enjoy it."

What? He wasn't even going to question her about her appointments? He was, apparently, holding his cards very close to his chest. Maybe he was seeing his own attorney. Maybe this was going to be dirtier than she had hoped. What a shame if he dragged this out into a nasty drama in front of the whole town.

"What was your day like?" Doris asked more innocently than she felt.

"The usual. Owning a construction company isn't as glamorous as you may think," he said and then chucked at himself.

Yes, Doris thought, *pretend you're all relaxed and don't have a care in the world.* She had never realized how fake Frederick could be. If he could so successfully hide his inner turmoil of their divorce from her, what else could he be hiding? Who was this man she had been married to practically all her life?

Doris drained the rest of her wine. She could cry right now— her nerves were so exhausted—if she had been a lesser woman.

"Can I refill your glass?" that conniving worm asked.

Doris nodded. She would need more fortification if she were to get through the days until the art show. She thought of the art show while Frederick was refilling her glass. It would have to be even more spectacular now. At first she had just needed the diversion from her horrid painting, something for the people to concentrate on instead of her art, but now it would have to be even greater so everyone in town would be amazed at her real talent. And even though Frederick would most likely not attend, he would not be able to avoid at least hearing about her stunning success. Doris suddenly felt better. Thank God for Daniel. She had no idea how long she would have lived in this misery if he hadn't come to town and opened her eyes. Though painting on canvas did not, in any way, interest her, his arrival had given her the diversion, the stepping out of her routine that she needed so she could acknowledge her unhappiness and accomplish this unavoidable deed. Daniel's gentleness, his interest in her struggling art, and his taking his time away from the store to listen to her—all that, she realized now, was more than she could ever expect from her insensitive slug of a husband. She was certain now that Daniel's arrival in Gilmont had to be the crutch she would need to stand up to Frederick and his attorney. Daniel would be there to help restore her after the crash. Because of Daniel, she wasn't alone.

"Well, you look pleased about something," Frederick said, handing the glass of wine to her.

"Just thinking about a little project I'm working on," she said.

Frederick stood and finished his scotch. "I'm starving. We eating in or out?"

"In if you want leftovers and out if you don't. I'm afraid I was too busy today to cook."

"Come on. Let's go out. Neither of us feels like dealing with making a mess in the kitchen."

Doris sipped her wine. "Why don't you just run out and get yourself something? I'm not really hungry."

Frederick scowled. "Really?"

"Really. Just go and don't worry about me."

Frederick hesitated, staring at her like she was some unknown person to Him. "I'll just make a sandwich," he said and went into the kitchen.

Doris got up and went upstairs to her room. She got comfortable on her chaise lounge and sipped her wine, watching the evening light out her window change the distant mountains from green to smoky blue. She was never one who believed in self-pity, but right now, tonight, she almost felt frail, on the verge of being some vulnerable victim in a cheap romance novel. She blamed Frederick.

Daniel had agreed to close the store early on Friday and give the women one extra day to work on their paintings. One by one they straggled in. Doris came first. She was quiet tonight. She asked for assistance in setting up her easel and getting the cap off her turpentine can, but other than that, she went right to work without a fuss.

Caroline came next. She looked a little out of sorts. When Daniel questioned her, she said that she was just getting over a little stomach upset. She'd had it for a couple of days—nothing contagious, she was certain, but it did take the wind out of one's sails. She knew she had a lot of work to finish on her painting, so she needed to come and make the effort.

Pauline breezed in next. She was anxious to get right to work. She had been thinking about this painting and had a little surprise twist she wanted to add. What did Daniel think of stripes—not wide or prominent like the other shapes, but stripes that were just almost there: pale, shadowy lines running down the painting like whispers behind the bold colors? Daniel was intrigued.

Eleanor came right behind Pauline. Eleanor opened her paint box, closed her eyes for a moment, and just breathed in. She relaxed her shoulders and smiled. This was just what she needed. Besides the fact that her painting needed a lot more work, she just needed to get out of her house and escape to this refuge. Also she had been reading her Bible and hoped she could talk to Daniel about some things that confused her. She hadn't seen him since their Tuesday class when he shared the story of his wife's death, and to be honest, she half dreaded bringing all that back to him, but he, of all people, would be able to help her.

Twilight came in. Everyone stopped painting. Who was this? Is this what Twilight looked like under all her camouflage?

"Well, look at you," Doris said, coming around her easel and standing in front of Twilight. "What happened?"

"I've been asked that everywhere I go. I guess I wasn't as invisible as I thought."

"Well, this is a pretty obvious change. You know," Doris said, cocking her head and examining Twilight, "apparently you can be attractive."

Twilight blushed and asked everyone to call her Elizabeth.

"Oh, thank God," Doris said. "I have wondered what kind of parents would name their child Twilight."

"That was self-inflicted," Elizabeth said. "But I'm afraid that I'm still as confusing to my parents as Elizabeth as I was as Twilight. They think I have become some religious fanatic now. They want to put me in therapy."

Daniel stepped up to Elizabeth. "Is there anything I can do? Talk to them, maybe?"

"Thanks, but I don't think that is necessary. They just need time to adjust. I mean, look at me. Sometimes I don't understand how I could have changed so quickly myself. I just know that I have. Tuesday when I painted that angel, and then when you told us about your wife, well, it was like a door opened, and I'm free. I don't think I have ever really known happiness before now. My life had truly been somber even when I was a little kid. Even before I let myself slip into my dark period. I mean, I really don't remember just feeling like this. I don't remember waking up optimistic about the day rather than just facing that I had to get through it."

"Wait. Wait. Wait. Are you telling us that because of that angel in your painting, you are now totally different?" Doris asked. This kid was exhausting. No wonder her parents wanted her in therapy.

"I guess that is what I'm saying. I mean I spent the night with my grandmother, and we talked all night about her faith, and so that helped, but it was really like a little miracle happened to me when I added the light to my painting. And since then I just can't stop thinking about God and reading about him."

"I don't know," Doris said. "Maybe you better slow down. Everyone has faith, but not everyone goes crazy about it." Doris paused and apologized for the word *crazy*.

Elizabeth nodded. "I'm sorry. I'm just so happy to finally be . . . happy."

"And we are happy for you," Doris said. "But we all have work to do, so it's back to the pears for me."

Order was restored to the class as everyone picked up their brushes and returned to their artistic struggles. Daniel moved among them, helping here, suggesting there, and correcting the angle of light on Doris's fruit basket. Everyone had settled into a concentrated silence when the door suddenly sprang open, and Ruthie barged in.

"Sorry I'm late, but it took me forever to get someone to finish my shift at the Bar & Grill," Ruthie said, stripping off her coat and heading into the back room to get her paint box and easel. "It's not like I haven't helped out everyone in the restaurant at one time or another when they needed time off."

Daniel disappeared into the back room to help Ruthie carry her supplies out. "I'm glad you could make it. I think this painting is your best, and I'd hate to have it not ready for the showing."

Ruthie stopped, a dead stop like she had run into some invisible wall. "Really? You, Mr. Professional Artist from Boston, think my painting is good?"

"Does that really surprise you?"

Ruthie shrugged. "Yeah. My paintings look kind of... I don't know, like shadows. Like a suggestion of something real, but not where you can actually see what they are. I keep trying, but this is the best I can do."

"Well, trust me, they are really something. Don't change what's working for you."

"Okay. Okay. Thanks." Ruthie carried her paint box and easel into the front room and started setting up her work area. Daniel might have thought he was helping her with his encouragement, but to be honest, he had just made everything harder for her. Before, her painting was just what it was. She just kept going with it because she didn't know what else to do. She truthfully didn't know what she was doing, so she didn't know what to change, and she was just fine with that. But now, Daniel thought it was actually good, and she could somehow change it if she wanted to—whoa, that was another whole level. She hoped he hadn't jinxed her, and now that she might actually try to be good, she would mess up whatever it was he had liked. Life just never got easier.

Class was almost over when Ruthie finally put down her brush and noticed Elizabeth. "Hey, girl, what's with the new look?"

Doris groaned.

Elizabeth shrugged. "It's actually my old look. Just decided to be myself again."

"Well," Ruthie said, "that's always a good thing. Unless.. ." She paused and giggled. "Unless you're me, and then being yourself isn't necessarily a good thing."

"Why do you always say things like that?" Carolyn asked.

"Like what?" Ruthie said, turning to Carolyn, surprised that Carolyn had actually said something. Carolyn never spoke.

"Like saying that being you isn't a good thing," Carolyn said.

"Well," Ruthie said, "take a short stroll in my shoes, and you wouldn't have to ask that question."

"If things are so bad, then why do you always seem happy?" Carolyn persisted.

Ruthie thought about that. Everyone paused in their painting, waiting for her answer.

"I guess," Ruthie said, frowning at her canvas, "if you expect everything to go wrong, then when it does, you are ready for it, and it doesn't disappoint you as much. You already knew it would be like this."

"That doesn't make any sense," Doris huffed. "How can you live if you expect everything you do to go wrong? What's the point of that?"

"No point, I suppose. Just easier," Ruthie said.

"Easier?" Doris was thoroughly annoyed now. "Failure is never easier. Do you realize how much effort it takes to keep fixing things that go wrong?"

"There you go," Ruthie said, shrugging a little. "I never try to fix things."

"What about your girls?" Carolyn asked, withdrawing as soon as she spoke, because she knew she had spoken what she should have only thought inside her mind.

Ruthie teared up instantly. Carolyn had hit that one tender spot still left after a lifetime of moving on.

"Oh my, I'm so sorry. Really, Ruthie, I'm sorry."

Ruthie stiffened her back. "Sometimes I have actually made decisions that were better for other people than they were for me."

"Of course, you have," Eleanor said, walking over and lightly touching Ruthie's arm. "You don't fool us with that tough-girl front. You are a big softie, and we all know it. Right, ladies?"

Everyone agreed, and they all moved silently back to their paintings. Daniel gave them a few minutes to let it go and settle back into their rhythms, then he walked over to Ruthie. "If you ever need someone to talk to, I'm always available," he said.

Ruthie looked up at him, her thoughts obviously on her girls. "Do you have children?"

He nodded. "Their mother got custody when we divorced."

Ruthie relaxed. Somehow that made her feel better, not that Daniel had felt the pain of that deep loss, but there was some comfort in knowing that she wasn't alone.

"Thanks," Ruthie said, "but I think I'm okay."

Daniel nodded and left her. She knew now that she was going to invite her girls and their father and even stepmother to the showing. Daniel had praised her work, so maybe there was something good there that her girls could see. And then out of the blue, Carolyn had brought up her girls when no one had ever mentioned them before. Well, that was definitely God sending her a sign that it was time to reach out. Maybe this God thing could be a good thing after all.

Everyone sighed a collective sigh when the class was finally over. It had been a long day, and this extra effort, artistically and emotionally, had left them all satisfied, but weary. One by one they cleaned and organized their tools and carried them into the back room. They all dutifully thanked Daniel on their way out—all except Eleanor, who had dawdled a little longer over her cleanup. Eleanor finally carried her canvas into the back and leaned it up to dry with the other paintings. She didn't know how to approach this quandary with Daniel, but for some reason, it wouldn't let her go.

"Are you all right?" Daniel asked, coming up behind her as she stood staring blankly at her painting.

Eleanor startled at his voice. "Oh, sorry," she said. Then she turned and faced him, her uncertainty evident on her face. "If you have a few minutes, I'd just like some help with something. Something I read in the Bible."

"Well, I am no apologetic," Daniel said, "but I will try."

"What is an apologetic?"

"Someone who has studied their religion to the extent that they are competent enough to explain it, to justify their faith, to others."

"I see. Well, I'm sure my question isn't that complicated."

"Let's sit, and I'll see what I can do."

So they sat on the crates, and Eleanor began. She told him that she had read the parable of the prodigal son—several times, in fact— and she still couldn't get it. As a mother especially, you know how mothers are with trying to raise their children to do what is right? So, of course, Eleanor couldn't get over the way the father welcomed his son home, had been looking for his return, actually, and then rewarded him when he had been so selfish. And then to add insult to injury, the father had told the good son to accept the way he was apparently rewarding the bad son. "I just thought that God was always watching us, judging our behavior, really, and he would not want us to reward, well, bad behavior."

Daniel nodded, understanding her confusion. "Let's start with what a parable is. It is simply a story told to teach a moral or religious lesson. Jesus used this parable to teach about God's grace and mercy. It's about God's unconditional love and forgiveness. When Jesus was telling this parable, he was talking to the Jewish leaders as well as the Jewish crowd. The Jews would be as appalled as you were that, first, the son was not immediately disinherited or even, in those times, stoned to death for his insult to his father. And then once the son had taken his inheritance and squandered it on having a good time, he would never have been allowed to return. And then to add the ultimate insult, the son had been tending to pigs to survive, and this was the height of humiliation since the Jews, according to the Old Testament dietary laws, considered pigs unclean. I mean, everything the younger son had done was unforgivable to the Jewish crowd."

Eleanor nodded yes—yes, that was what confused her about the father's behavior.

"But," Daniel said, "the son had returned to his father in a remorseful and humble state, and the father had given him what he did not deserve, which is grace, and he did not punish him as he deserved, which is mercy."

Daniel paused, and Eleanor just had to ask why, even though the father did not turn the son away, did he actually celebrate his return?

"Because his son had been lost and now he was found."

"Well, he wasn't actually lost," Eleanor corrected him. "The younger son had left on his own, remember? I have to agree with the older son, who had stayed home and done everything the father had asked. I would have been angry that the younger son could just stroll back in and be treated so ... so forgiven."

"And that brings us to God's unconditional love and forgiveness. When we stray, when we make mistakes, whatever they are, God is always waiting, watching for us to come back to him, and it doesn't matter the condition we are in, he will welcome us with open arms and give us robes instead of rags and sandals for our feet. He will celebrate because we were lost and now we are found."

"But the older brother. Is there no justice for him?"

"The older brother was the Jewish leaders who believed that they were due God's rewards simply because of the religious works they did. They didn't understand that Jesus was promising to change that. Human works alone can't earn salvation. The youngest son had nothing to bring back to the father, he had done nothing good with his life, and yet God still wanted him. That was Jesus's message."

Eleanor sat still, thinking about this. She finally nodded. "Okay, okay, I think I get it."

"Good, because getting it means living it."

"What?"

"We are the hands and feet of God on earth. We need to live with the grace, mercy, love, and forgiveness that we ourselves have been given. Being a Christian is a way of life that fills our souls and touches others."

"Oh my. I never thought of it like that. I mean I always thought of myself as a Christian, but that was always, you know, a personal thing. It wasn't something that I felt I should actually do anything about. I mean I wouldn't know what to do to be the hands and feet of God. That is so overwhelming."

Daniel smiled and patted her hand. "You're a good woman. I'm sure you do many things that please God."

Eleanor still looked a little worried. "It was easier before . . . before you told us about your wife and the angel."

Daniel agreed. So many things were easier before that night. But now that he knew what believing meant, he had to live it. "Well," he said, standing up, "I guess that is enough to think about for one night. Are you feeling good about your painting?"

Eleanor was grateful for the change of subject though she was the one who had asked him for the biblical explanation. Still and all, it felt, at times, like quicksand—the more you got into it, the more you couldn't walk away from it.

"It's late," Daniel said. "Let me lock up, and I'll drive you home."

Eleanor protested that it wasn't far, and she would be fine, but when he said nonsense, it wouldn't be out of his way, she gratefully accepted. The darkness had never troubled her before, but lately, she had found herself leaving lights on in rooms she wasn't even in. She could hear Bill in her mind, scolding her for the waste of electricity, but she just brushed him aside; if he hadn't died and left her alone, she wouldn't need the extra lights.

Chapter 5

Ruthie sat at the kitchen table, sipping her hot coffee and staring into space. Friday night had turned out to be busier than she had expected, and she was still beat this morning. She just wasn't bouncing back like she used to. Maybe she needed to see a doctor about a checkup. Or maybe she was just getting old. How old would she have to be before she could just keel over and give up?

"Well, it's about time," Max said, coming into the apartment with his arms full of grocery bags and kicking the door closed behind him with his foot.

"Shut up, Max," she said.

Max chuckled and dropped the bags on the table. "Love that crazy curl on the top of your head."

Ruthie scowled and reached up and smoothed something lumpy back down.

"Are you up for solid food yet? I bought fresh doughnuts from the diner."

Ruthie nodded. He knew she could never refuse warm nutmeg doughnuts with her coffee. If she wasn't still groggy, she might have suspected Max to being up to something. He wasn't exactly a morning person either, and many a Saturday they had argued over who would go out and get food.

"You stay and party after work?" Max asked.

Ruthie accepted the doughnut box he extended but growled that she hadn't been drinking; she had been working. "Besides," she said, "how would you know when I got home? You were sound asleep with the TV still blaring."

Max conceded that was probably true, but he did know that he had been awake when the late news went off, so he knew she had come in after that.

"When did I have to start answering to you about when I get home?"

Max laughed out loud and went to work, taking care of the refrigerated items.

Ruthie dunked her doughnut into her coffee and bit into the soggy dough. Ahh, she did suddenly feel better. Had her mother ever made fresh doughnuts? Was this a memory or just something she liked for itself? She couldn't remember her mother much, so it must be just for itself.

"I'm thinking of taking the bike out for a ride today. You want to come along?"

Ruthie glanced at the clock. One o'clock? Seriously? One o'clock in the afternoon? "Why didn't you wake me up? It's one o'clock. The day is almost gone."

"Well," Max said, taking care of the canned items now, "I thought of it, but then I remembered that you didn't have to answer to me about when to get up."

"Go to hell, Max."

"Probably, I will, sweetie, but not because you send me there."

Ruthie dunked another piece of doughnut. "I've been thinking about the art show."

Max crumpled the plastic grocery bags and stuffed them into one hanging on a nail inside the pantry.

"I've been thinking about inviting my girls to come and see my paintings."

"Okay."

"But—and I don't know why I'm even talking to you about this—but I am—afraid."

"Afraid they will come or afraid they won't?" Max asked.

Ruthie looked at him standing there in front of her. "I don't know. Both, I guess."

Max kicked back a chair and sank down into it. "You can't hide from them forever. I didn't know you when you last saw them, what, three years ago?"

Ruthie nodded. Suddenly, her throat hurt.

"They may just be hoping you contact them as much as you want to. Did you ever think of that?"

Ruthie shook her head.

"Look, when is this big art showing?"

"Wednesday afternoonish . . . evening," Ruthie squeaked out.

"Great. Call them."

"I need more coffee," she said, and Max got up and refilled her cup.

"You drink this, and I'll go dust off the Harley. After you make your call and do something with your hair, come and get me, and we'll take a short ride. It's cool out there, so layer up."

Ruthie nodded.

Max poured himself a cup of coffee and went out. Ruthie stared at her cup. When was the last time she felt like crying? She couldn't remember. What was wrong with her? Was she starting menopause? That made her crack, and she giggled. *Poor Max,* she thought.

Okay, okay, she had to get a grip on herself. A phone call was the only way. It was too late to send some scribbled note and expect them to get it in time to make plans to drive the thirty miles over just to look at a few blurry paintings. Maybe this was silly. What did they care? They had lives she didn't even know about. Maybe Wednesday was their busy night. Maybe it was a family night, like sitting around the kitchen table, the rest of the house dark and quiet, eating large Pizza Supremes, and sharing stories of their successes and dreams. Okay, now an actual tear did escape and roll down her cheek.

Ruthie sat her nub of doughnut down and got up from the table. She looked at the phone and then went to the door. "I can't," she said. "Max, I can't do it."

"Just do it."

Ruthie closed the door. Of course. She had done so many difficult things in her life. What was this? A phone call. She would center herself, and as she had explained to the women, if you expected nothing, then you wouldn't be disappointed when you got nothing. So here goes nothing.

Ruthie picked up the phone and punched in Robert's cell number. She didn't have to look it up because she had secretly been tempted to call him many times, and so by now, she knew the number by heart. His phone rang three times before he answered it.

"Robert," she said before he had a chance to wonder who the call was from. "It's Ruthie."

There was a pause, and then he answered, "Ruthie, what a surprise."

"I know. But there is something I wanted to ask you . . . something I wanted to invite you to, actually. Well, not you if you are not interested, but maybe the girls could come if they had time and wanted to come. It's nothing really important. Just something I was thinking may be nice. Something that wouldn't take a lot of time or any commitment, really. Just drive over and back, and that would be the end of it. If that is what they want, of course."

"What is it?"

"Well, now don't laugh, but I have been taking painting classes, and we are having a little showing of our paintings on Wednesday. And I was hoping if you and the girls are free—and Linda too, of course, if she was comfortable and wanted to come—then you could just pop over and see what I have done and then scoot off again with no strings or complications. I promise. I will not act like I expect anything. Just maybe come and then leave, and that is all."

The phone was silent as Robert thought about it.

"Seriously, I understand if you don't think it's a good idea. I have tried to stand by what we agreed, but this isn't really interfering in their lives. It's just a few minutes, and then it is over."

"They have been asking about you lately."

Ruthie sank down on the couch, her chin trembling as she waited for the rest of his answer.

"I'll ask them. What time and where is it, in case they want to come?"

Ruthie gave him the information and thanked him a hundred times and hung up the phone. Then she just sat there on the couch, her hands knotted in her lap, trying to recover.

"Well?" Max asked, coming back in.

"He's going to talk to the girls and let me know."

Max smiled. "And now about that hair?" he said.

Ruthie and Max rode the back roads, the cold air stinging their faces. Ruthie clung to Max as he opened it up on the flats. She probably had bugs in her teeth from smiling so much. What a beautiful day. The dry autumn leaves littering the road scattered with their speed. Fields blurred as they flew by. If Max ran into a tree right now, Ruthie wouldn't care. She would die happy.

Saturday mornings in the fall found Frederick sitting like a lump in front of the TV, watching college game-day shows. Really, year after year after year, he watched people just sitting there behind a little box, talking about football. How much could there be to say when the game hadn't even started yet? And still, there he was listening, nodding, and making faces when he disagreed, like any of that mattered in real life.

Doris finished cleaning the kitchen from lunch and then gathered her notebooks and headed up to her chaise lounge. She could sit there without the distraction of that babble and work on her plans for the art show. No one could even imagine how much work really went into an event like this.

Doris opened her notebook; she had ordered the banner for the street. It had cost extra for the colored letters and the decorative border, but she didn't care. She had thought of listing all the women's names on the banner, but some of them might deter people from coming instead of enticing them. So she left the names off and would let everyone just be surprised.

She sketched out a layout of the room—where the food and beverage tables would be and the section of the room that each artist had to display their work. Doris snickered; she still couldn't use the word *artists* seriously with these ragtag women, but that didn't matter. This wasn't really about the painting anyway. Next she listed the food she wanted and what serving platters she would need. Then she noted which items could be made the day before, or at least prepped, and which could not be assembled until the last minute. Next she needed a grocery list for each food item and then what she had available and what she would need to shop for.

She knew she had enough tablecloths but would need to buy more candles and fresh flowers. It was fall, so she would do it all in amber colors. Daniel wanted lights shining on some of the paintings, so she would have to get with him to see how they could work that out. Of course, there was no problem she could not solve. It was just a matter of knowing what was expected and getting it done.

Doris sighed and lay back against the lounge. A sudden shadow of worry fell over her. What would she do after the art show? She knew she wouldn't continue to paint. Good grief, that was obvious. But what would she do then to fill her time? Frederick would be served the divorce papers on Thursday, so she wouldn't even have him to deal with. What did sixtyish women do all by themselves? Maybe she would travel, go to places she had seen in her magazines. She wasn't afraid to fly. She wasn't afraid to explore new things on her own. She could almost see herself in Morocco—long colorful dress flowing as she strolled the market streets, picking up exotic things, haggling with the vendors, and stopping among the noise and chaos for herbal teas. Or maybe France. Oh, how she had always wanted to go to Paris. She would be so at home there among the beautiful streets and beautiful people. She would shop—a hat was a must— and sip burgundy wine at a little table on the street corner. She could almost cry when she thought of all the wonderful places that being married to Frederick had deprived her of. Thank God, she had come to her senses before she was too old to make up for her losses.

Doris nodded. She was okay now. She stood up and gathered her notebook and pen. She started toward the door when she noticed Frederick standing there. "Oh my," she said. "I didn't expect you."

"Just wondering where you disappeared to."

Doris was instantly suspicious. Frederick had never checked on her before. Why, he hardly knew if she was even in the house most of the time—well, except for mealtime. Oh yes, he was interested in her then. "Do you need something?" she asked.

"Not really," he said then noticed her notebook. "What are you working on?"

"Don't worry, it's nothing you have to be involved in."

Frederick nodded. "Okay," he said and started to turn and leave. Then he looked back at her. "Is there anything you want to talk about?"

"What?"

"Well, I've noticed lately that you have had something on your mind and thought you might want to talk about it."

"Seriously? In all our years together, you have never asked me to tell you what was on my mind. Why now?" Oh, Doris knew why he suddenly was showing an interest in her thoughts. He knew about the divorce and wanted to confront her about it. Well, too bad. She wasn't cracking.

"In all our years together, Doris, I have never had to ask you what was on your mind. You were always generous with sharing whatever it was, but lately . ." Frederick shrugged. "Well, never mind."

Frederick seemed sincere, maybe even disappointed. How dare he pull this on her! But still there was something about him at this moment that she felt obligated to please. Oh, why was he always able to manipulate her like this? She had always, since high school even, been vulnerable to his rare moments of interest in her. She caved. "I'm just planning an event. You know how involved that can be. It takes a lot of preparation."

"The art show?"

Drat, she had hoped he didn't know about that. "Yes, but don't feel obligated to go. It's really just a little something Daniel wanted."

"I saw the posters in the store windows. Wednesday, isn't it?"

"Yes. But I know that is your poker night, and honestly, it isn't going to be anything you would be interested in."

"Are your paintings going to be there?"

"Frederick, really, why all the questions?"

Frederick just looked at her. She felt her face growing warm under his questioning eyes. She had to get away before he weaseled everything out of her, before she weakened and blabbed about the divorce papers being prepared for delivery, and before she weakened and went back to wanting him to love her.

"I was just on my way out to do some shopping. I know you will be in front of the TV all day, so now is a good time to get some things taken care of." Doris looked away from his face—that face that never seemed to age from the young, confident—well, arrogant, actually—face she had schemed to claim for her own. Why did he have to look like that? Why did he have to look at her like that? Doris forced a smile. "I shouldn't be gone long," she said and breezed past him, pleased with herself for her show of strength in the face of his manipulating fakeness.

Doris left the house with Frederick settled back in his favorite TV chair. Her hands actually trembled a little as she turned the steering wheel to back out of the garage. For all the reasons she already had for leaving that man, he had now added a new one—fake caring. Thank God, she wasn't the type of weakling to crumble into his arms at the first hint of fake caring and lose all self-respect.

Doris parked on Main Street and wandered in and out of the shops. She was buying more than necessary, but she didn't care. She deserved nice things. She had a reputation to uphold, and this was going to be spectacular. She had even found canned sea urchin roe that appeared very interesting. She didn't ask any questions from the clerk when she paid for it. For one thing the clerk was barely out of kindergarten, and another was that she was not about to admit she didn't actually know what she was buying. She'd do some research and impress with it.

Doris continued down the street. She found disposable napkins that one would think, at first glance, were fine linen. She paid for them and had to stop and wonder who, besides herself, in this backwoods town would ever purchase anything like this. No one entertained like she did.

Doris eventually ended up at Daniel's store. Daniel was actually helping a customer. Edith Tanner was buying an art book of some sort for her granddaughter's birthday. "Never too young to expose them to the arts," Edith said as though she knew a flit about the arts. Doris knew Edith, and she wasn't fooling anyone with this fake artistic sophistication. Fake. Fake. Why was everyone but Doris so fake?

"We will see you Wednesday," Daniel said as Edith left the store.

Doris was just relieved to have her gone. "I've brought the floor plan for the art show," she said, pulling her notebook out of the big bag she was carrying. They walked over to the counter, and she opened to the page she had sketched.

Daniel studied it. "You've done a wonderful job. I'm certain the other artists will be pleased with what you are doing to showcase their work. But the cost of all this. It may be more—."

Doris stopped him. "I'm taking care of it all. No reason for anyone to worry about it. I'll need some physical help on setting everything up, but that would be all."

"That's very generous," Daniel said.

"Yes, well, I will have the details all ready when we meet Tuesday for our last class. Then I can assign everyone an area to help with. I have ladies who will help me with the food. You may remember them from your grand opening."

Daniel assured her that he did, indeed, remember them, and then they got to work figuring out the lighting. Finally, Doris slapped her notebook close and slid it back into her bag. She was getting ready to leave when she remembered that tomorrow was Sunday and asked if Daniel would be interested in going to church with her. Frederick never went, so Daniel wouldn't have to worry about him. Daniel thanked her but said he went to the Presbyterian church out of town.

"Why, aren't they all the same, really?" Doris was anxious to get Daniel to her church so she could be a part of exposing his miracle story.

"They are all God's churches, yes, but the reason there are different denominations is because some formats suit people better than others. It's all about what works for you. I have been to many churches that were beautiful, the sermons were uplifting and inspirational, but I left them as I would a great theater show. Pleased—that I had been, but not exactly moved spiritually. I had to look around and find the right fit for me."

"Well, maybe I could go with you someday. See if I get spiritually moved."

"Hopefully, you are getting what you need where you are, but I'd be pleased to take you with me tomorrow if you want to see," Daniel said.

"No, no, I can't go tomorrow because I'm expected to sing in the choir. I have a solo, actually, and then I am hosting a small women's luncheon."

"Then another time," Daniel said.

Doris nodded and then asked him if he was thinking of telling his priest or pastor or whomever about his wife's angels. "Seriously, don't you think that would be interesting to religious people? I mean, they, over anyone, should be interested in angel sightings."

Daniel agreed that yes, religious people should be interested in angel sightings. Then he watched as Doris glided out of his store, a woman full of confidence and contradictions. Sometimes God must get a good chuckle out of some of his creations.

Eleanor could hardly bear the wait, and yet she dreaded the wait to be over. At least she knew what her life was like now, but sometime today her daughter, and God only knew who else, would be pulling into her driveway, hauling all of Trish's belongings from her strange life in Florida. Trish had only been home about once a year since she had left, and then it was . . . uncomfortable. She came in like the haughty princess she had been when she left. Neither her mother nor father had gotten any smarter in her absence. She liked to sleep most of the day and roam around all evening with the riffraff she had rounded up from her high-school days. She usually stayed a week, and then they would drive her back to the airport, her father slipping her money, her mother slipping her money, and off she would go for another year. Eleanor wondered if she could handle this without Bill. At least the two of them had dropped into their respective chairs on their return from the airport and just looked at each other, understanding without saying a word how the other felt. That look had been, at least, a little comfort. They would sit awhile in the silence, and then Bill would say, "Well, let's get back to it, then." And their life would resume as it had been except for the awakened weight of disappointment and, of course, the loss of hope that followed Trish's visits. Eventually, they moved past it and slipped back into their quiet routines.

Eleanor wandered through the house, soaking in the calm and order while she could. She had started her day reading about the prodigal son. She knew now what was expected of her, but she didn't know if her heart was healed enough for the mission. She knew her heart was not as pure and forgiving as it should be. She was sorry about that. Hugging Trish was like forcing herself to hug a cactus. Neither she nor the cactus wanted the contact. Still, she knew what she must do. God had given her Trish as she had prayed, and it was her duty to love and forgive her. It was her duty to welcome her home with her best fatted calf and open arms.

It was almost three o'clock when Eleanor saw the silver convertible pulling a small U-Haul trailer rumble into her driveway. Eleanor stood up from the table and straightened her spine. She would be happy. She would be happy. She would be happy. Eleanor went out on the back porch and down the steps to the convertible. There was no strange tan man in the car with Trish. Eleanor relaxed. Good. This would be easier. Then as she approached the car, she stopped—dead stopped. Trish hadn't brought home a man; she had brought home a tiny baby in a car seat. Eleanor stood confused for a moment as Trish got out of the car and came around to her mother.

"What a trip. Never, I mean never, make a twelve-hundred-mile trip alone with a one-month-old."

Eleanor looked at her. "Why didn't you tell me, Trish?"

"Oh, you know how you are, you would have wanted to come down, and things were complicated enough."

Eleanor didn't hug the cactus; instead, she went to the side of the car and looked down into the baby seat. That sweet round face, perfect tiny lips, and closed eyes fringed with dark lashes. The chubby baby hands lying on the pink blanket.

"I named her Ella."

Eleanor looked at her daughter.

Trish smiled. "Yeah, after you. What do you think?"

Eleanor shook her head. "I had no idea. She's beautiful. She is such a surprise."

"Well, our little surprise is about to wake up, and then we will see what you think."

Trish opened the passenger door and tipped the seat forward. She gently unsnapped the car seat restraints and lifted the little pink bundle out and handed it to her mother.

Eleanor curled her arms around the tiny person, and her heart hurt with the love she felt. She could never have dreamed. Maybe she had thought of this moment and had hoped for this moment the first few years Trish had been gone, but she had stopped thinking about it for some time now.

"Better get inside," Trish said. "When Ella wakes up hungry, the whole neighborhood will know she has arrived."

Eleanor carried the baby up the steps and into the house while Trish grabbed her purse and the diaper bag. Eleanor sat down on the first chair by the door and just stared at the tiny face as it squirmed and struggled to wake up. This was the most precious thing Eleanor had ever seen. She was overwhelmed with a flurry of emotions. How did one instantly grasp the thrill of seeing their first grandchild when they had given up hope of ever having one?

Trish washed her hands and then came to take the baby. "I'm afraid you can't help her with this, but after I feed her, you can have her back. I need to crash. The last few miles were a struggle to stay awake."

Trish woke up for dinner and held the baby as her mother cooked and then cleaned the kitchen. Over dinner Trish did say that Ella's father was a no-show. He hung around and pretended he was interested, but by the end, he had just disappeared. Trish was grateful, really. He had been fun, but she had always known he would never be long-term.

"After all these years," Eleanor said, "how did this happen?"

Trish shrugged. "I had to stop the pill for a while. I was having problems with it. But I was using other methods. Who knows? Things happen."

"Do you think he will come back . . . and want her, I mean?"

Trish shook her head. "He isn't the type. I'm sure he has moved on and forgotten all about us."

"I can't imagine such a life," Eleanor said, "having children and then walking away. How does a man, a woman, live like that?"

"Oh, Mom, you have no idea," Trish had said, and Eleanor was grateful she didn't have any idea of such a life.

───⁓∘⊙⟨⊙⟩∘⁓───

Disappointingly, Fran had been taking a nap when Trish had arrived. Fran was careful not to stray far from the front window since seeing the convertible and U-Haul. Fran hoped they hadn't taken in all the suitcases so she could, at least, catch a glimpse of whomever Trish had brought home. She would bet her house it was that slick foreigner who was way too old for Trish.

Fran walked along the front windows into the kitchen to get a cup of tea and go sit on the front porch. It was a little chilly for sitting outside, but she'd take one of Milly's ugly afghans for her lap. The tea was made, and Fran was making her way to the front door when the phone rang, startling her so that she slopped the hot tea over the rim of her cup and onto her hand. She cursed and wiped the hot tea onto her dress. That reactionary mistake did not please her either.

Fran sat the cup on the telephone table and picked up the receiver. "Hello," she barked, letting whoever it was know she was not pleased with the interruption. If someone was calling to sell her a funeral plan or an extended warranty for her new car, she was really going to tell them what she thought of their intrusive and unwelcome calls.

"Fran, what's wrong?" Milly asked.

"Well, it's about time I heard from you. I was beginning to think they had you locked in the basement away from any form of communication." Fran didn't know where that had come from, but it perked her up a little to imagine Milly knitting away in the gloom and solitude of a dank basement as they pushed her meals to her through a small doggy door. For a moment Fran even forgot about her burn or the tea stain on her dress. She couldn't hold it in; she actually snickered at herself. She had obviously been watching way too many old horror movies.

"Anyway," Milly said, "I thought I should let you know as soon as possible that I won't be coming back. Well, I will be coming back to get the rest of my things, but not actually moving back."

"What?"

"Yes, the kids helped me find a small apartment near them, and it is in a nice neighborhood and close to the shops and—"

"What do you mean you are not coming back?"

"I mean I'm going to be living near my family. The rent is subsidized. It's based off my social security and—"

"I don't care what it's based off. How could you just up and go off and do something like this behind my back?"

"It's not behind your back, Fran. Really."

"Of course, it is. Did you discuss it with me before you left? No. Did you tell me you were going to go there to find a place to live? No. Did you even let me know when you started looking for an apartment? No. It is definitely behind my back. And after all I have done for you."

"I know. I'm sorry. I didn't really plan it. I just wanted . . . well, to give you a break from me, and then the kids told me of this—"

"For the past five years your kids have done nothing for you. They haven't even wanted you around, and now they suddenly need you near them?"

"Yes," Milly said, not arguing with Fran about any of it.

Fran felt blindsided. She was speechless. She was suddenly overwhelmed with the ingratitude, the unmitigated treachery, the . . . the . . .

"Fran? Fran? Are you there?"

"Of course, I'm here. It's you who isn't here."

"I know," Milly said meekly.

"I won't take you back if you leave. Do your precious kids know that? I won't have you running in and out of my home at their whim."

"Yes. We know."

"Good. Fine. So long as you know I won't be treated like this after all I have done for you."

"Yes, thank you."

Fran was done with it. There was nothing left to say. "When are you coming for the rest of your things?"

"We thought maybe Sunday. Afternoon."

We. We. Milly was suddenly a *we?* "Fine," Fran said and clunked down the phone. Fran stood there a minute just staring at the phone. She couldn't believe Milly would just up and do this behind her back. Why? Could any subsidized cracker-box apartment possibly be better than this house? Was Milly going to be better off doing everything for herself? Could she even do everything for herself? Was there not one brain among those fidgeting oblivious imbeciles that could see what a disaster it would be for Milly to try and live on her own?

Well, that was all their problem now, not hers. Fran picked up her tea and turned from the phone to the front door. She started toward the door and then remembered she needed to get Milly's afghan for her lap. Fran intended to go get it, but instead, she stood there, by the door, just absorbing what had happened, then she went to sit in her favorite chair. Was Milly really moving out?

Elizabeth was sitting at her desk in her room, finishing up an English paper, when she heard a light knock at her door. She got up to open it and found both her parents standing in the hall. Her mother asked in a gentle voice if they could come in. Elizabeth stepped back to allow them to enter. Elizabeth's father looked around the room, seemingly inspecting everything. Her mother sat on the very edge of the bed, hands clasped in her lap.

"What?" Elizabeth asked.

"Now, dear, don't be upset," her mother began, "but I was, sort of, bringing your clean clothes up to your room yesterday and happened to discover these two books. I wasn't snooping. I just happened to notice them when I was in here taking care of your clothes." Her mother pointed to the books Daniel had loaned her that were on the bedside stand.

"Okay," Elizabeth said, still waiting for the reason they had come to her room.

"Well, we discussed it, and we are wondering if there may be something you want to talk to us about."

"Can you be more specific?"

Her father stepped up now. "Elizabeth are you . . . ill?"

"What? No. Why would you think that?"

"Well, these books are about people's deaths," her mother said. "One seems to be by a hospice nurse, and the other, about a doctor dying and going to heaven and back. Are you afraid you are going to die? I mean in the near future rather than when you are old? Is that why you are turning to God now because you are afraid you may have some terrible disease?"

Elizabeth relaxed and smiled at them. "No. No. There is nothing wrong with me. I'm fine."

"Then why?" her mother asked.

"Why the books?"

Her mother nodded.

"Here, Dad," Elizabeth said, patting the bed beside her mother, "sit down, and I will try to explain."

Elizabeth turned her desk chair around to face them and sat down. She started with the painting classes, how she went in to Daniel's shop out of idle curiosity, but he had approached her as if she were there legitimately, and they had talked, and somehow she had ended up asking him if she could join the class he was putting together. Didn't they remember she had asked them for class money? They said, of course, they remembered; they had agreed that that type of activity would be good for Elizabeth, maybe allow her to see the beauty in life again.

"I wanted to paint, but my paintings came out dark and . . . and depressing, really. Until . . ." Now Elizabeth smiled and shook her head at the wonder of it. "Until I, for some reason I don't even know, I added white to the dark room, and then even more bizarre, I painted an angel floating up in the corner of the room."

Her parents scowled. They loved this child dearly but had, much to their constant heartache, not only never understood her, but they might also actually be a little frightened of her strangeness.

"That's nice," her mother said in an effort to be supportive, but really, she didn't see how adding white paint to a dark canvas could lead one to reading books about dying. Didn't death have more to do with darkness than light?

"The books, Elizabeth," her father said.

So Elizabeth explained how the class had reacted to her painting and how confused she herself felt when she realized what she had done. And then to top it off, Daniel had told them about his dying wife seeing angels in the corner of her room and being ready to go with them to heaven.

Her father shook his head. "I'll return the books today and discuss this with Daniel. I'm afraid you will probably be finished with painting classes for now."

"No," Elizabeth said. "Mom, please, no."

"Oh, Sweetie, we will go to church with you if you want. If that will make you feel better. But we just have to take this opportunity to help center you."

"Center me?"

"Yes, we are thrilled you are finally leaving your black everything, but. . ." Her mother paused, stopping herself from using the phrase "normal children," and instead just said that young people could get confused and move from one extreme to another. "You are working so hard to figure out the world that it can be overwhelming. We want to help you."

"I have to finish the class. We have an art exhibit in a few days. I want to show my paintings. . . now."

"Elizabeth," her father said, "we are your parents, and I believe"—he said, glancing at her mother as if they had not always agreed about what was best for Elizabeth—"that it is time for you to concentrate on getting the best grades you can in your senior year and start picking a college. God and the devil can wait until you graduate, and then you can figure it all out as an adult."

"But God is winking at me NOW," Elizabeth pleaded and then realized by the look on her father's face she had made a great mistake. "I don't mean that the way it sounds. I just mean that something in me changed when I painted that angel. Really, it did. I want to do my best in school, but I can't stop this. If you just let me finish the showing, it's only a few days away, then I promise I will buckle down and concentrate on college."

Her parents glanced at each other. Elizabeth could feel the tug of war. "Please, Mom," she said, turning to her mother. "Just a few more days and I will put my painting aside. I promise."

Her mother looked away from her father. "Okay. We will give you until after the art show, but then we will talk again. And in the meantime, I think we would both feel better if you didn't read any more books about death."

Elizabeth wanted to explain that the books were not about death; they were about real people believing in life after death—a whole other wonderful idea. But of course, her parents' minds were closed to the subject. "I'll take the books back on Monday after school."

"Just for the record," her father interjected before they left Elizabeth's room, "I would like to return them now myself."

"Just a few more days," Elizabeth heard her mother saying as she closed the door behind them. Elizabeth returned to her English paper, but she couldn't concentrate. God wasn't like a favorite toy that could be randomly taken away for bad behavior. God was real and lived inside her now. How could she separate from that just because her parents chose not to understand?

Elizabeth closed her eyes and pressed her hands together. She did not know how to pray, but she needed to ask for help. "Please, God, I believe in you. I can feel how you have changed me. Please, help me convince them that you actually touched me. That a miracle happened to me. I want to believe in heaven. I want to believe that you watch over me. I don't want to lose you." She stopped and opened her eyes. She didn't know what else to say. She didn't even know if her prayer was real. All she did know was there was so much more to learn about God, so much more she couldn't stand not to know.

⚬⚬⚬⚬⚬⚬

Eleanor lay in her bed, straining to hear through the walls. Was Ella awake? Were they in there cooing baby talk to each other? Did Ella have her silky little pink hand wrapped around her mother's finger? "Oh, Bill," she whispered and wiped at the tear running from the corner of her eye. "I'm afraid."

"Mom," Trish whispered through the closed door. "You still awake?"

Eleanor answered that she was, and her door opened. Trish and Ella came and snuggled into Eleanor's bed. Only the hall light lit the room, but Eleanor could see Ella's little dark eyes wide-open.

"I haven't figured out how to teach her the difference between day and night. She sleeps all day and then wants to stay up at night."

"Hmm, wonder who she gets that from," Eleanor said.

"Please, God, don't let her be me. I'm happy to be me, but I don't want to have to try to love a me."

"Are you admitting it wasn't easy?"

Trish pushed up on her elbow and grinned. "I can't say I ever did anything intentionally to hurt you and Dad, but I will admit that there were probably many times you two were not pleased with me."

Eleanor put her face close to Ella and breathed in that sweet, powdery baby smell.

"Mom, I am sorry. Truly. And I'm sorry to come home like this now. No husband. No job. A brand-new baby. I know it isn't what you expected ... or I guess it is probably exactly what you expected but just hoped against."

"Trish, I'm your mother. I only want the best for you. And with or without a husband, I'd say you have the best right here. Everything will work out. You'll see."

"I have to admit that I thought about abortion. It would have been so much easier. I'd just do it and then get back on with my life just the way it was. But I couldn't do it, Mom, I just couldn't actually do it. Abortion sounds okay as a word, but when you think about what it really is ... I realized I just had to finally grow up and start doing the right things. And now, when I see her, and she is beautiful and real ... I actually cry that I ever, even for one second, thought of killing her."

Trish stopped talking, and Eleanor reached over the cooing baby and laid her hand gently over Trish's hand. "I'm proud of you."

"Oh, Mom, what am I going to do?"

"Stay here. Get a job. You have a reliable babysitter. Meet the perfect man, and get married."

Trish laughed and then sighed. "In our dreams, right?"

"That's where good things start."

"I'm sorry, Mom, you don't need all this hassle."

"You have no idea how much I have needed all this hassle."

"Oh my! Oh my, Ms. Ella, what did you just do?" Trish said after the bubbly diaper explosion changed the conversation. Eleanor and Trish laughed as Trish scooped up her smelly baby and exited the room. Trish started to close the door, but Eleanor asked her to leave it open.

"Okay. Good night, Mom. And thanks."

Eleanor lay back against her pillow—so much to think about, so much to be grateful for. Maybe Jesus was right—welcome them home no matter the brokenness of them, no matter the shame they had to carry, and no matter the new burdens. Just open your arms, and hug that cactus with all your strength. This was a second chance for them both, and maybe this time they could get it right.

Eleanor was alone in the kitchen when she heard the knock on the back door. She sat the blueberries back on the counter and went to the door. It was as she had feared—Fran. "Good morning," she said more graciously than she felt.

"Good morning," Fran replied, bustling in out of the cold. "Trish won't be driving around with the top down on her convertible today."

"I suppose not," Eleanor said. "Can I help you with something?"

"No. No, just brought over some of last year's strawberry jam. Thought you could use a little extra with your company and all." Fran walked into the kitchen far enough to glance through the doorways into the other rooms. "Guess they must still be in bed."

"I heard them up."

"Good. Well, it's good we have a few minutes. I wanted you to know so you wouldn't wonder when you don't see Milly around anymore."

"Oh my, what happened?"

"Her family happened. I'm afraid that it appears her family has brainwashed her into thinking she wants some shabby, run-down little apartment near them over coming back here to a perfectly comfortable home. I mean it's never been my place to tell her what to do, but this just seems wrong. Something just isn't right. She ups and unexpectedly goes off and then mysteriously decides not to come back. Maybe . . .," Fran said, wrinkling up her old face with a frown, "maybe she came into some money somehow, and those kids want her close enough to get their greedy hands on it. I don't know, it's something. Something stinks about this."

"Well, I can see how you would worry about her, you two have been living together for, what, four, five years?"

"Five years and seven months to be exact," Fran said. "I took her in when no one else wanted her. I was living my life. I didn't need her aggravation. But it was the right thing to do. No one can accuse me of not putting myself out there to do the right things."

"No, they can't," Eleanor said, adding in her mind that Fran always did the right things as long as they were what Fran decided were the right things. "Well, I'm sure you're going to miss her."

Fran harrumphed about that and predicted that it would be Milly who regretted her decision. "I told her that I wasn't having her moving in and out. If she leaves, then she is gone. She better be sure, when she gets here today to pick up her stuff, that she is one hundred percent sure she wants to leave, because when the door slams behind her skinny butt, then that is it. My generosity can only be stretched so far."

"I understand," Eleanor said, totally understanding. "Well, thanks for coming over to let me know. I will definitely watch for her so I can go over and say good-bye."

"Oh, you will hear them for sure. If her whole brood comes with her, then everyone on six streets over will know they are here."

"Sounds like a boisterous bunch. Things will certainly be different for her," Eleanor said, inching back toward the door, hoping to say goodbye to Fran now.

"I don't expect them for a while. I have time for a coffee if you have it ready."

How does one hide the aroma of fresh brewed coffee? "Please sit down. I'll get you a cup."

Fran obliged and was rewarded with not only a hot cup of coffee but also the appearance of Trish and a baby.

"Well, well, now look at this. Who is this little princess?" Fran said, suddenly transforming from her cranky self to her happily surprised self. A baby was even better than that old foreigner.

"Hi, Fran. This little princess is Ella."

"Ella? That's an unusual name, isn't it?"

"Actually, I named her after Mom. I love it."

"Well, that's another surprise, right, Eleanor? That Trish would ever name her child after you. I mean the way you two have always been out of sorts with each other. I'd have expected her to name her child, if she ever had one, after some, I don't know, South American celebrity she drove around to bars in Florida." Fran chuckled at her own wit.

"Looks like surprises abound today," Trish said. "First Milly and now Ella."

Fran drew her face back at the mention of Milly. Why did Trish have to spoil the fun by bringing up Milly?

Eleanor interrupted their tit for tat. "I'm just finishing up blueberry muffins, Trish, if you can wait for them to bake. If not, I can fix you whatever you want."

"I'll wait. Ella is fed and happy, so I can enjoy a cup of coffee and wait for my mom's fresh muffins. Ahh," Trish said, "it is good to be home."

Well, Fran knew right then and there that something wasn't right. What was Trish trying to pull?

"So how long are you home for?" Fran asked.

"Maybe to stay. We will see."

"Really? What happened in Florida . . . well, I mean besides a baby?"

"Actually, a lot happened in Florida—a lot good and a lot bad— but all in all, I can come home feeling okay about it."

"Well, where is the father?"

Trish shrugged. "Guess I'll have to find one for Ella."

"Well, do you even know who the father is?"

"Of course."

"Is he that old man you brought back for your father's funeral?"

Trish grinned at Fran. She had forgotten how much fun Fran could be. "No. Carlos was just a very good friend who offered to come with me. He knew Ella's father wouldn't, so he came with me in case anyone discovered that I was pregnant, and then he would, you know, stand in as her father. Mom had enough on her plate at the time. She didn't need my problems."

"I knew it!" Fran said, beaming. "I knew you had put on a lot of weight for someone completely obsessed with her appearance."

"Well, good for you, Fran. Always one to be on top of things."

"So who is the father?"

"Dwayne Parker."

"Well, that doesn't mean anything. Why isn't he with you and his daughter?"

Trish sipped her coffee then sighed and looked right at Fran. "Now, Fran, wouldn't that be my business, not yours?"

Fran frowned. That Trish had always been insolent!

"You know, Fran," Trish said, "I overheard you and Mom talking, and I was wondering if, when Milly's family comes to move her out of your house, if maybe they could help me unload the U-Haul."

Fran sat her half-empty cup down and stood up. "I need to get home."

"Wait," Trish said. "You haven't even finished your coffee or told us what you did to make Milly choose her supposedly horrid family over you."

Fran looked back at them when she reached the door. "Enjoy your jam, Eleanor," she said, and then she was gone.

"Trish!"

"What? Come on, Mom, that woman is fun to mess with. Don't try to tell me that you never felt like giving her a dose of her own medicine."

Eleanor smiled and reached out to take Ella. At least for this day, she had this precious sweet-smelling tiny person, plus her daughter back, plus Fran on the run. Who would have dreamed!

Daniel was raking leaves when Elizabeth's father pulled into his driveway. Daniel leaned the rake against the maple tree and walked over to greet him.

Elizabeth's father left his car and came to extend his hand and introduce himself.

"What can I do for you, Samuel?"

"I'd just like to talk about my daughter and . . . well, things she told me about her painting class."

"Certainly, come on inside."

"Thanks, but this shouldn't take long."

"Then let's get to it."

Samuel swallowed and stuffed his hands into his pockets. "She said you told her that your wife saw angels."

"That's right."

"Why would you do that to a girl who is obviously struggling with her identity?"

"Because it's true. And because Elizabeth is ready to explore her faith."

"Don't you think her parents are the ones to determine what she needs?"

"I feel we need to be frank here," Daniel said. "Where your daughter was and where she is now should be a comfort to her parents, not a problem. And believing in angels isn't something unnatural. I told her about my wife's experience because something amazing happened to Elizabeth that night, and I knew she was ready for God to enter her life."

"She is ready to just be a normal teenager, who should be thinking about college and not reading books about death and painting supernatural pictures because she thinks she was guided into it by some spiritual something."

"God would be the spiritual something you are looking for. Look, I don't know your beliefs, and I'm not judging because I was just like you before my wife's death, but Elizabeth believes something beautiful happened to her that night, and you should be grateful she is looking for God instead of demons."

"That isn't the point. The point is that when you are paid to teach painting, you should be teaching painting, not preaching."

"I can't agree with that. Including God in everything we do and touching every life we can with His love is what we all should be doing. I believe my wife saw angels, I believe she is in heaven, and I intend to live my life so I can be there with her and take as many other souls with me as I can."

"I'm sorry about your wife, and I can see how you need to feel like that. But Elizabeth is only eighteen. She has a lifetime to figure out what she believes. Right now she just needs to be a ... regular kid, damn it!"

"I understand," Daniel said. "I do. Of course, you want what is best for her, but let me ask, have you seen her paintings?"

"No."

"How about we go to my shop and see them, and then maybe you will understand what I am talking about."

"I don't see what difference looking at her paintings can make."

"But you will," Daniel said. "You will see."

Samuel stood in the middle of the art store as Daniel disappeared into the back room. He just wanted help from this man to finally direct Elizabeth into being a normal teenager before her opportunity was gone. He would gratefully welcome the problems other parents complained of if Elizabeth would just go out with her peers and commit the expected assortment of teenage antics.

Daniel came back into the shop with two canvases, both pointed away from Samuel.

"This first one is one that Elizabeth has not had time to correct. She has done three paintings, and two of them have been finished. She wants to get them all corrected before the showing on Wednesday."

Samuel shrugged. "I don't know what *corrected* means."

Daniel turned the first canvas around and sat it on the counter. He watched Samuel's face tighten, watched Samuel close his eyes for a moment. Then Samuel just whispered, "Oh my."

"Do you know where this room is?"

"My mother's house. And the little boy on the floor, playing by the bookcase, was my brother. He died when he was just five."

"There is a lot of sadness in this painting. The colors are somber, the expressions on the boy and woman are grim, and the person who painted this saw your mother's house like this."

Samuel nodded.

"Now look at this one," Daniel said and sat the corrected painting beside the other. "This is what she painted before I ever told her about my wife. This is why I knew I should tell her."

Samuel studied the painting. It was so similar to the first—his mother's house and his mother sitting in the chair by her Bible—and yet it was totally different. In both paintings, Elizabeth had put the picture his brother had drawn of the tree. In the dark painting the tree was bare and spidery, and in the other, it had white dabbed leaves on the black branches. There were touches of brightness all around the room—all coming from the direction of the angel up in the corner. The woman's face was softer in the second painting. Where the first woman definitely had the gothic look he had seen in Elizabeth's pencil drawings at home, that look that was, in all honesty, uncomfortable to linger on, the second painting made you want to keep looking at her face. How did Elizabeth do that?

"Aside from the topic you are here to talk about, I have to say that your daughter has talent. I know a lot of artists, it's been my business all my life, but I have never seen anyone do this. With just a few precisely placed touches of white, she has transformed a painting that haunts you with its sadness to one that makes your heart feel hopeful. Elizabeth was actually surprised herself when she saw what she had done."

Samuel studied the painting. His eyes glistened with emotion. "I just want her to be okay. I want her to paint tulips or balloons or sunsets—just something pretty."

"God is working on her," Daniel said. "Trust him."

———⁘———

Doris left the ladies' luncheon after church, feeling like it was time well spent. She had entertained the ladies with stories of the art class. She didn't give names, of course, she wasn't that petty, but she couldn't help it if her descriptions were so precise that most of the ladies were certain they knew whom she was talking about. She hadn't been unkind, that was not her, but sometimes the truth just could not be dressed up. Let's face it—Carolyn does not have much to offer. She hardly spoke. She definitely did not make an effort to impress on any level. Everyone knew her husband was a pitiful drunk. Oh, he did his job at the nursing home; what was it—some type of maintenance, all-around, do-anything kind of menial position, but just do not drop by for a visit after he got home from work. And Doris had heard that he was drunk most of his days off. So with that type of homelife, why did Carolyn paint the most detailed flower-boxes-and-blue-shuttered-windows type of pictures? She would never have a home as cozy and perfect as she painted. You'd think that dwelling on the painting of such nice places would make her all the more depressed to go home to her shabby little house.

And Eleanor—she was a lost soul. At times Doris even thought that Eleanor held fanciful intentions toward Daniel. Here she was, a new widow, and yet Doris could not ignore the soft voice and fluttered lashes when Eleanor spoke to Daniel. Doris knew women, and she could see that Eleanor had a great emptiness that she was trying to fill. Look at her paintings for pity's sake—roads leading nowhere. How much louder could one scream that they were lost and lonely?

Then there was Ruthie. Good gracious, what was she thinking joining a painting class? She dressed like she thought she was still in high school or something—if she ever even went to high school. She had lived with every Tom, Dick, and Harry. Now it was some biker who tore through town like a speed demon trying to end it and not concerned if he took anyone else with him. They were middle-aged. When would they realize that they were not heading toward their life? This was their life. They needed to grow up and do something with it.

She did not leave Pauline out though she didn't know much about Pauline except that for such a timid soul, she painted with crazy abandon. Her paintings made absolutely no sense, but she did have a way with color. One could almost appreciate what she was doing if her paintings were not so weird that you had to look again and then again, hoping you'd catch something that made her work relevant to something in real life. Doris was afraid she could not understand the globs and swirls or the mind that envisioned them. How do you see that kind of art? Did Pauline know what she was going to do, was there actually a plan to her creation, or did she just start with a color and see what happened? Well, at least, from all that Doris heard, Pauline had a nice, normal family.

And speaking of normal or actually not normal . . . did any of the ladies know a skinny little waif who went by Twilight, or by Elizabeth at the moment? Well, that was one spooky child. She hardly said a word, which was unnerving in itself, but what she painted was actually something you would expect to see in one of those creepy vampire movies. If you looked at her paintings long enough, you'd guarantee yourself nightmares for certain. Well, of course, that was before her great. . . what would one call it? Out-of-body experience? No, what happened to her was definitely "in body." She appeared to change from the inside.

Elizabeth claimed that one evening when everyone was quietly painting, she had been visited by an angel with a gift from God. The ladies had gasped, which only encouraged Doris to break her promise to herself that she would not tell Daniel's story until he was ready to share it himself.

The more intrigued the ladies were, the more they leaned forward, totally taken in by this unbelievable story that Doris was sharing, and the more Doris couldn't stop herself until, in the end, one of the women insisted that she must retrieve the minister to hear about Jill's angels. Doris was forced to promise that she would not utter another word until the lady who was doing the retrieving returned with the minister.

Finally, after small talk and fidgeting, the minister did arrive with his escort. He was young, really, for such an important position, so Doris was doubtful of his contribution to the drama unfolding in the little room. Doris repeated her story in detail. The women listened as though they had never heard it before; so amazing was this miracle—didn't Daniel call it a miracle after all? Finally, they all sighed and sat back, looking now at the minister for direction.

The young minister set his lips and thought how to approach this. Finally, he just came out and said it. "I'm a little disappointed that all of you feel this is so unbelievable. Aren't you Christians?"

They looked at one another and nodded.

"Then are you saying that you think God has been out of the miracle business these past two thousand years? Once Jesus was resurrected and the apostles all martyred, then God left us on our own?"

They looked around the circle of confused faces. This was not what they had expected; even Doris was caught off guard.

"I am going to respect Daniel's privacy about his wife's death as I hope everyone in this room will do. I do, however, hope he decides to share his story with everyone he meets. Miraculous things happen to those who believe, and the more we acknowledge them, the more we are willing to share our God moments, then the easier it will be for everyone to accept the truth when miracles happen to them. I want you to all go home and think about a time in your life when you thought you had a stroke of good luck, but now realize that what you experienced was really God giving you a gentle nudge in the right direction. If you believe, and I know you all do, that is why you are here today searching for further growth in your spiritual journey, then you must believe in God's continued work for us. God loves us, and he allowed Daniel to get the comfort he needed in knowing that his wife is contentedly sitting in heaven, waiting to share the wonder of it with him. Can you even imagine how much easier that must be than for a nonbeliever who thinks his loved one is just dust in the ground?"

The women grew somber. They had never, in all their lives, thought of God like this. They were Christians, certainly, but going to church and doing bake sales for the missionaries and spaghetti dinners for the mourners' families was one thing; what had happened to them today was a totally new concept. They suddenly almost felt unworthy to be here listening to talk of miracles and God's love.

"Well," Doris said, "look at the time. I guess we better think about cleaning up. I know Frederick is wondering where I am."

The other women stirred and began gathering up the remnants of their luncheon.

"Oh, oh, oh!" said Doris before one of them could slip away. "Remember, I need your help with the reception on Wednesday night, and then I expect to see you back checking out the art exhibit."

"We wouldn't miss it," they all replied.

"And you too," Doris said to the minister. "I'll introduce you to Daniel."

"I look forward to it," the minister said and pitched in to help the ladies set up the room for the Monday night men's group meeting.

Unfortunately, Doris had to leave before the work was all taken care of, but she jokingly reminded them that they would be welcome to come on Wednesday to eat and look at art as long as they all promised on their favorite grandchild's head not to make one snide comment about her artistic talents.

———◦◦◦◦◦———

Milly, her son, and her grandson pulled into Fran's driveway in a pickup truck. The truck had Bondo patches on the green front fender. The rest of the truck was black. Fran assumed the patches were from road salt rust. Humph, guess none of them were bright enough to know that if they just washed the road salt off every now and then throughout the winter, then it would be harder for the salt to eat through the metal. Yup, the running board on the driver's side was rusting too. *Well, good luck, Milly,* Fran thought as she went to open the door before they could get there.

Milly came in first, smiling and actually looking a little perky. Had she started drinking behind their backs? Maybe in front of them. They wouldn't care.

"I brought pictures of my new apartment," Milly said. "Of course, it will be a month or two until the current tenants move out, but I'm first on the list. Rebecca works for the bank where the apartment owner works, so she helped me move up on the list."

"Well, that doesn't sound very fair to the other people on the list," Fran said.

Milly sat her big black purse on the telephone table and nodded. "I know. But apparently, that is how things work anymore."

Milly's son and grandson came in and stood by the door. "Hello, Aunt Fran," Milly's son said. "We are ready to get this done. May get rain later, and we want to get all Mom's stuff in the shed before that happens."

"By all means," Fran said, stepping out of their way and gesturing her hand toward Milly's room. "There isn't much. She moved here from a trailer, you know."

"Yes," Milly's son said, walking past Fran. "We know Mom's humble beginnings."

Milly followed the boys into her room and gave instructions on what they could take. "I'll get my things in the bathroom. Don't need you boys bothering with that stuff."

Fran waited, pacing around the living room as they made multiple trips in and out of her house, their cloddy big boots probably tracking in dirt. Finally, the deed was done, but Milly's son said that they would be a few more minutes as the young woman across the street asked them to unload her U-Haul before they left.

"Young woman?" Milly asked as the boys headed across the street.

"Trish is home," Fran grumbled. "With a baby."

"Oh, how nice."

Fran scowled at her sister as though she had lost the very last bit of sense she possessed. "Nice? What's nice about crawling home in shame and bringing your burdens back to dump on your poor widowed mother?"

"Oh, Fran, a baby isn't a burden. They are miracles. And I bet Eleanor is happy to have her family with her. I often worried that she must be lonely in that big house all alone."

"Really? You worried about Eleanor being alone, and at the same time, you up and leave me?"

Milly visibly withdrew. "It was time," she said, pleading for her sister to understand. "You know that's true."

"And how would I know that? Did you talk to me about leaving? Did we have one conversation about you skulking off and moving into some smelly little apartment by yourself?"

"It's not smelly. It's part of a retirement community, and there is a clubhouse and walking trails nearby and—"

"And none of that is the point," Fran snapped. "I want to know why you decided to do this without talking to me."

"Because," Milly said, looking away from Fran's angry face, "because I couldn't breathe here any longer."

"What? What the hell does that mean? Of course, you could breathe here. What kind of an idiotic thing is that to say?"

"Fran, please don't be angry with me. I was hoping we could still get along. I was hoping maybe you could drive over and visit me when I get settled in. It isn't really that far."

"You were hoping? Does everything have to be about you?"

"No, of course not."

"Well, don't hold your breath. When you leave, you are gone. I told you that."

"From your house, not your life, right?"

Of course Fran wanted to inform Milly that choosing to leave her sister's house was choosing to leave her sister's life. But then who would be left? Who would Fran have if she never saw Milly again? Fran felt trapped. Just like that, right out of the blue, Milly had found her long-lost family—that was not there to help Milly when she needed it most, one might add—and was now leaving Fran alone in this big house. How had this happened? How could one fix things if they weren't even aware they were broken? Oh, why couldn't she have had a normal, clear-thinking sister! Why hadn't their parents had one more child—another child like Fran that Fran could enjoy to live with in her declining years, someone Fran could count on.

"I don't know," Fran said. "I'm just so disgusted by the way you handled this I don't know what to do or think."

"I understand."

"Good."

Milly's grandson came up to the door and opened it. "Dad said we are ready to go. And the ladies over there insisted we take twenty dollars each for helping them and then gave us a few blueberry muffins for the trip home."

"How nice," Milly said. "I have always thought highly of Eleanor."

Fran grunted and went outside ahead of Milly. Fran stood on the top step and looked at that old rattletrap of a truck loaded with all of Milly's earthly possessions. *Good riddance,* Fran thought and felt a little better than a moment ago. She would be fine. God, how pitiful would she be if she actually needed Milly to exist? Yes, yes, she would be fine until Milly fell flat on her face and had to beg to come back. She understood that we were all meant to carry burdens, and Milly was hers. So of course, Fran would have to take her back in no matter how rudely Milly had left or how annoying she could be.

Milly paused and awkwardly leaned in to hug Fran. "Thanks. I really appreciate everything. Really."

Fran let Milly hug her and then watched her go down the steps and get helped up into that death trap of a truck, where she was stuck in between those two large boys most likely reeking from sweaty work, and then Milly smiled foolishly and waved as they backed out of the driveway. Fran stood still as the truck pulled away, hillbilly music blaring, and then she went to sit in the swing. She would go and see what her house looked like with Milly gone in a little bit. For now it was a beautiful day, chilly enough to feel good on your skin, but warm enough to keep you outside. Or maybe she should go in and open some windows and let fresh air into the house so she could breathe.

—⁓∽⌀◦∾⊙⊹⊙∾◦⌀∽⁓—

Elizabeth stopped by her grandmother's house on her way home from school on Monday. She ran up the steps and opened the door. Her grandmother was not expecting her, and yet the door was not locked. Gram always said that if someone wanted to get her, they would find a way in. "Locked doors only keep out honest men," she would say.

"Well, well, now look who's here," Gram said, coming out of the kitchen, drying her hands on a green checked towel.

"I'm on my way to the art store. I have to return some books and work on my last painting. I only have two more nights to get it finished for the showing on Wednesday. But first, I want you to tell me more about Jesus."

"Always happy to," Gram said. "Just let me finish a few things in the kitchen."

Elizabeth followed her grandmother into the kitchen and sat down at the table as Gram scraped the chopped carrots off the cutting board and into her pot. "What specifically do you want to know?"

"Well, these kids at school have invited me to join their Christian group if I want to be a follower of Jesus, but I don't know what that means. Shouldn't we just be followers of God and then also, you know, know about Jesus and what he did while he was on earth?"

"That would be the case if Jesus was just a prophet. But Jesus is God. The Trinity is the three ways God has chosen to communicate with us. He has spoken to man directly as we talked about in the Old Testament, but that wasn't the only way God tried to reach us. Sometimes the direct approach still escaped man. As no one could see God in a physical way, He sent His son so we could see Him and know how God wanted us to live. So God sent Jesus, His Son, a part of Himself, to actually live among us. And we know that Jesus was not the whole of God, because if He was, then Jesus would not have prayed to His Father. So the Son was another way God chose to reveal Himself to us. Unfortunately, even in human form, we simple people chose not to understand God's will. So when we still resisted the first two approaches, God sent us His personal voice. The Holy Spirit is God's little voice in our heads. When we truly believe, when we accept Jesus as our Savior, then the Holy Spirit comes alive, and if we listen to Him, He will guide our hearts."

Elizabeth thought about that as Gram wrapped up the carrot-and-potato peelings in the old newspaper she had used to catch them. "So," Elizabeth finally asked, "following Jesus is following God?"

Gram nodded. "Do you have time for a piece of pie?"

"If you do," Elizabeth said. "I don't know why I've been so hungry lately."

Gram was pleased. Elizabeth certainly could do with putting on a few pounds. "So do you think you would want to join this Christian group?"

"I want to, but I have to wait awhile. My parents are a little freaked out about my sudden interest in God."

"Well, now that isn't right."

"It's okay. I understand. But what I don't understand is why I painted what I did."

Gram sat the two pieces of apple pie in front of them. "What was that?"

"You and your house. Only I painted them very dark and sad."

Gram cut off the tip of her pie and frowned about that.

"I'm fixing them. I'm making them brighter. But I don't know why I saw your house like that. I know I was feeling dark when I painted them, but I don't know why I tried to paint your house that way."

"I'm sorry you felt like that about my house."

"Well, of course, it wasn't your fault how I felt. It was all to do with my self-imposed gloominess. But now that I'm coming here, and we are talking about all this, I don't know why I used to be . . . so unhappy here."

Gram sat her fork on the side of her plate. Gram knew. She knew when Elizabeth changed. Her parents had been over one afternoon, and Elizabeth was coloring at the dining room table. The adults were talking about the latest miscarriage Elizabeth's mother had suffered.

"We are giving up trying, Mom," her son had said. "I'm going to get the operation. We can't go through this again. We don't have the strength to keep losing our babies. It's become easier to just accept that we will never have another."

His mother had protested. She said that, perhaps, they just needed to see a specialist and find a reason for the miscarriages. It could be as simple as hormones or, maybe, a minor surgery of some sort.

Elizabeth's mother had broken down weeping, and Elizabeth had turned in her chair. "I have to concentrate on the one child I have and forget the dead ones," her mother had said.

"You have dead children?" Elizabeth had asked, leaving her chair to join them.

"Of course not," her father had said. "You are our only child, and you are very much alive."

"Then why is Mommy crying?"

"She is just sad . . . just sad about . . . about Gram's little boy who died. Remember we told you about him? He was only five and got really sick and died. That still makes us sad."

Elizabeth's mother had gotten up and fled from the room. Her father followed, and Elizabeth and her grandmother just looked at each other as they listened to the two voices down the hall. Elizabeth's grandmother could see the trouble in the child's little face. Elizabeth's eyes darted to the picture her son had drawn and then to her grandmother and then toward the voices crying and pleading. Gram had known that Elizabeth needed more than that as an explanation, but when she would ask her son about how they were handling it, he just said that they felt it was best to ignore the subject and Elizabeth would eventually forget about it. But Gram knew Elizabeth was not a forgetter. Elizabeth had a serious little heart, and she wouldn't let the image of dead little brothers and sisters go. And apparently, that worry, that sadness, had fallen on Elizabeth each time she had entered her grandmother's home.

"Well, I am very pleased that you don't feel unhappy any longer when you come here."

"You're going to come to the art show, aren't you? I want you to see what I have done. I hope you will like my paintings."

"Now, if they are paintings of me, then I hope you used some artistic license and made me look a little younger and maybe a few pounds thinner."

Elizabeth smiled. "Oh, Gram, I'm not that good a painter. No one but us will even know it is you."

"Then I shall surely be there."

They finished their pie, and then Elizabeth had to dash off to return some books. Gram followed her to the front door to say goodbye again and then walked over to the table by her chair. She picked up her son's drawing and touched her finger to the pale pencil marks he had so long ago drawn with his chubby little hand. Maybe they had been right. How do you explain the pain of this to a child?

Elizabeth was surprised when she got to Daniel's shop that there were so many people there. There might be one or two at the most, but the art shop was not a highly trafficked store. Daniel smiled at her when she entered and motioned for her to go right in the back and get to work.

Finally, one by one, the women left. Some bought a little something, and some just browsed, glancing at Daniel as though he had newly appeared in their midst.

Daniel came into the back when the store was empty. "How is it going?"

"This one is harder. I think I'm ready to move on to something else."

"Like what?"

"Oh, I don't know. Just not this anymore. I think it must be easier to paint light than to try and pull it out of darkness."

"You are entirely right. But these three pieces work now that you have changed them. I think, after the show, we could even send them to a gallery I know and see how they do."

"That would be awesome, but what is the point? What if I can't paint like this anymore? What if these are paintings from my gloom, and I don't have it anymore?"

"The talent is there, or it is not. Gloom can come and go, but it can't create artistic talent. You will discover what is right for you in time."

"Yes, first I have to get going on my grades. And I have to return your books. I've read them both, but my parents want me to take a break and concentrate on school. I guess I have worried them enough. I have to try to wait, but to be honest, the more I know about God, the more interesting He is. I mean, the Trinity is brilliant."

Daniel laughed. "Yes, it is. Did you like the books? Did they help at all?"

"Oh yes, I guess one of the biggest questions is if heaven really exists. How great it must have been for that doctor to actually have gone there and come back. I mean, what could ever happen to you in your life again that could make you be afraid?"

"Indeed," Daniel said. "Indeed."

⁓⁓⦿⦿⦿⦿⁓⁓

Ruthie sorted through her closet. Did she even have anything to wear to the art show? What did one wear to such a thing? She had never needed to know because she, honest to God, never dreamed that she would even be going to one, much less be showing her own paintings. And worse yet, the art show was in the very town she worked in. Who could take her art seriously when they already knew her?

Well, her girls were coming, and they didn't really know her. They might actually take her seriously after seeing her there presenting her art. Daniel said her stuff was good, so she could relax about that. Oh, it wasn't anything great, just dabs and dashes of paint that sort of looked like something. Still it was more than she ever, in her wildest dreams, thought she could do. Even Max was getting into it, asking what type of paintings she had done. She told him not to worry about it; she hadn't done any nude male portraits. Ruthie laughed at that.

But seriously, her girls were coming, and she had to look right. They were modern teenage girls, so they would know fashion. All Ruthie's clothes were old rags! Rags! Ruthie had to go shopping. First she would stop at the drugstore and peruse through the magazines to see what fashionable women were wearing today and then hit the shops. She probably needed to get her hair colored and reshaped— well shaped. She could always do her own nails. She even had some of those flowery stick-ons that would dress her nails up a bit. Ruthie looked at her nails. She was a waitress! Who could expect a waitress to have fancy nails or even nails of any length? Slinging dishes and slopping water and cleaning coffeepots did not pamper one's hands.

Ruthie flung herself back on the bed. It was too much. She hadn't even seen her girls, and already they had changed her life. She suddenly felt inadequate on every level. She accepted that she had been an inadequate mother, and now she was admitting that she was an inadequate dresser, and . . . she didn't even have decent nails. Ruthie stared at the water-stained ceiling above the bed. This was when she would normally jump up and put on her clown outfit— figuratively, not literally—and go out and act up. She might go to the diner and heckle whoever was there, customers and co-workers, or go to the Bar & Grill and schmooze someone into buying her a drink. She had to modestly admit that she was hard to resist when she really threw herself into it. But Ruthie groaned and rolled over; she didn't want to schmooze her girls into liking her. In fact, she thought what she wanted was to stop schmoozing everyone. But how could she? If the funny, happy Ruthie suddenly disappeared, who would be left? Just some dabs and dashes of a person. People would be able to see she was a person from a distance, but when they got up close, they would see she was just a colorful blob—no definite character or worth.

Ruthie was still languishing on the bed when Max got home from work.

"Ahh, turned into a lady of leisure, have you?"

"Leave me alone," Ruthie said; she was even feeling too low to tell him to go to hell.

Max dropped his lunch box on the table and sat down to unlace his boots. "Funny thing, you asking me about where I would live if I ever left here."

Ruthie was a little interested. She propped herself up on one elbow and waited.

"Looks like the crusher plant is moving to Linton."

Ruthie sat up. "Linton? Like Linton, Vermont?"

Max chuckled. "I assume that's the one."

"Well, are you going with it?"

"What else is there for me to do here?"

Ruthie got up and smoothed her bed-mangled hair. "When are you moving?"

"In the spring, I expect. We will be shutting down here at the first snow."

Ruthie paced. "I thought, maybe, you'd like to go to Barbados if you ever left here."

Max pulled his tired feet out of his boots and tossed them into the corner. "Barbados? Woman, are you crazy? Could you get me a beer while you're flitting all over the place?"

Ruthie opened the refrigerator and got him a Budweiser. "So, Linton," she said.

"Yep."

"You know my girls live in Linton, right?"

"I do."

"You may not like Linton. It's kind of quaint. Kind of a backward little place."

"Like here?"

Ruthie found herself by the corner where his boots were tossed, and she bent and sat them up straight. Normally, she would have yelled at Max for flinging his dirty boots all over the house, but today she didn't feel like it.

"Linton, huh?" Ruthie said.

"Yup. You thinking of moving with me?"

Ruthie looked surprised. "What? I just heard about it. How would I know what I want to do in the spring?"

"True. True," Max agreed.

"You know," Ruthie said, wanting to change the subject until she had the time to really chew it over, "I don't think I have one decent thing to wear to the art show."

"Well," Max said, grinning like a fool, "I've always been pleased to see you naked, but I'm not sure the whole town will be."

Now Ruthie had to tell him to go to hell.

Max drained the rest of his beer and got up. "Guess I'd better go wash some of this sand off before it gets stuck in all my cracks."

"Don't clog the drain," Ruthie said.

Max headed toward the bathroom then stopped and turned to her. "Why aren't you out buying something nice instead of wearing the paint off the floor? I don't know of anyone who is going to show up at our door with the perfect dress for you."

"Then I guess you don't know everything," Ruthie said even though she knew it didn't make any sense. Her mind was still on Linton, so she wasn't up to her best at comebacks.

Max chuckled and proceeded into the bathroom.

"Besides," Ruthie went to the bathroom door and spoke loud enough for him to hear, "I have to be at work in an hour. How do you expect me to find a dress in an hour?"

"By trying," he said back at her.

By trying? Now that had always been her weak spot. That Max knew just where to hit her when she was down. She didn't know why she even put up with that fool. But seriously, maybe tomorrow she'd better try to find something. She could, maybe, squeeze in some time between the diner shift and her last painting class before the show... before the show and before her girls came. *Oh god!*

⁓⁓⦿⦿⦿⁓⁓

Pauline hummed as she set the table with her good china. The kids and Tim would think she was crazy. Here it was just any Sunday night, and she had cooked a beef roast with all their favorite sides. The kids loved her corn casserole, and Tim was always begging her to make her double-baked potatoes. They were a pain with the cooking and scooping and chopping and mixing and rebaking, but she felt good about the smile they would bring. She had taken the time to make buttermilk biscuits and put out her homemade apple butter in a crystal dish. She added her autumn cloth napkins and amber water glasses. She had even stepped out the back door and clipped some wild black-eyed Susans for the center of the table.

There! It was finished, and she felt better than she had in a long time. While Tim was watching football and the kids were playing outside with their friends, she had disappeared into the attic and finished her third painting. And she loved it. She just loved the way the three worked together. What a gift it was to have the sheer joy those paintings gave her and then to have this wonderful family and home. She stood with her hands on her hips, admiring and appreciating, and then, though she had never thought to do it before, she even gave a silent prayer of gratitude to God. For some reason it felt right to thank him for this moment. The world was fragile, nothing could be taken for granted, and one should try to constantly be aware of wonderful moments and acknowledge them. *Thank you, God.*

So when Tim really, really wanted to eat in front of the TV because the game was too close to leave and the twins didn't want to come in just yet—couldn't they just have thirty more minutes, just thirty? The Reynold's mom gave them thirty more minutes—Pauline fixed Tim a tray and wrapped two plates in foil to keep warm in the oven. Then she sat at her place at the table, lit a candle, and moved the flowers closer to herself. And she even put Pandora on a soft-music station. Pauline forced herself to relax, to feel the beautiful music, to close her eyes and breathe slowly, and to take dabs of her lovingly prepared food and position them carefully onto her blue wedding china. She cut a small bite of beef and studied the black-eyed Susans. She had never thought of using those colors in her paintings. What could she do with yellow and brown? She pulled one of the flowers out of the vase and laid it on the blue bread plate. Yes! She could see it now. She could paint a flower if it was bold on bold—just that beautiful yellow on the blue. And to think some had questioned her for picking such basic dinnerware? Blue? Just all blue? Ha! She had been right. Admittedly, at the time she chose it, she was picturing it on a snow-white tablecloth with white napkins and white frosted glasses. But now it was obvious she had a deeper reason, an artistic reason. For the first time ever, she realized that her mother was right; she had always loved color, always saw it as more than a round circle of blue.

Pauline pushed her chair back and picked up her cell phone. She closed Pandora and called her sister.

"Hi, Patricia, it's Pauline."

"What's up, munchkin?"

"Well, not much, actually." Pauline paused. It was hard to sound important to an attorney who had her house on the golf course decorated with real art by real artists. "Basically, I just wanted to call and invite you to an art show this Wednesday."

"Okay. Anyone famous?"

"No. Sorry. Not yet."

"So . . ."

"Actually, it's . . ." She paused and almost said *only,* but this wasn't an *only;* it was important and big. "It's a showing of local art. From a class I have been taking, actually."

"I see," Patricia said. "So you have paintings in an art show?"

"Yes."

"Great. And it's this Wednesday, you said?"

"Yes. I know this is short notice, but well, to be honest, I have been wrestling with myself whether or not I should bother you with it."

"Bother? Please. I'd love to see what you're doing. Where is it going to be?"

Pauline told her and asked if she could go by the nursing home and pick up their mother.

"Sure," Patricia said. "It should be fun. What are you painting?"

Pauline felt a sudden hesitation. Maybe she had gotten too full of herself. Maybe she had only painted kindergarten shapes of color after all. Maybe it wasn't real art. No, no, she would not back down—not this time. "It's hard to describe. Just come and tell me what you think. And please be honest."

"That is never a problem for me. Just remember that you asked."

"I will. So great. See you Wednesday."

"Wouldn't miss it."

Pauline closed the call. Well, now it was done. She had actually invited her sister to the most important night of her life. Certainly, Pauline had had important moments—her wedding, the birth of her twins—but then there had been distractions at her wedding, and there was the arrival of two new lives for everyone to focus on, where this night she would truly be naked before the world. This showing of her art exposed her inner self for all to see. She had never felt this alone. No one—not Tim or her mother or even Daniel—could protect her from the truth of her work. It was either as exciting as she thought or as foolish as she feared.

"It's not a contest, Pauline," Daniel had said. "It's just sharing what you do, what you see."

Daniel was right. Of course, he was right. She had to let go of caring what her sister might think of her. Pauline couldn't honestly say that she loved everything Patricia bought as art and put up on the walls of her home. Pauline would just show what she loved and . . . nothing. She'd just present her work.

Pauline picked up the flower and cradled it gently in her hand. It was so basic, just petals around a center—so simple yet beautiful. If she did not have all this mess to clean up, two kids to get fed and bathed, she would escape to the attic and start a new painting. She would see what yellow and blue would feel like.

Chapter 6

On Monday Doris shopped for the food for the show. Normally, she would be perking with enthusiasm over the perfection of her details and her impending great success, but today she carried a weight—the weight of Frederick! The attorney had called her this morning to go over a few details, and it had totally unnerved her. Of course, she was going ahead with the divorce, and of course, she needed to do it, but that wretch she was married to was making it so much more difficult than it had to be. Why, this morning, before the call, he had glanced over his paper when she had set his breakfast in front of him and actually smiled at her. When was the last time Frederick had smiled at her? That jerk!

Doris pushed her grocery cart down the produce aisle. Were there no decent fruits and vegetables grown in the world anymore? Look. Just look at these cucumbers—shriveled on one end and greasy with wax. She couldn't make anything beautiful out of these, to say nothing of the taste. They would all be bitter. She could tell by the look of them. And these cherry tomatoes! Impossible!

"Doris, hello."

Doris glanced up to see Pauline. Doris nodded and forced a smile. She was never one to be rude even though she might be busy and out of sorts. It wasn't Pauline's fault Frederick was so horrid.

"Do you have a moment?" Pauline asked.

Actually, Doris didn't have a moment to spare on drivel, but she could not forget who she was and the obligation she had to be gracious to others. "Certainly," Doris said. "Is there something I can help you with?"

Pauline shrugged. "I don't know exactly, but I get the feeling that I have missed something important that happened when I left class that night Twilight, or Elizabeth rather, painted the angel, and everyone stayed but me to hear what Daniel had to say."

"Oh, that night. Let me see," Doris knew what Pauline was referring to, but she just didn't have the time or patience to get into it right now, so she just casually said that all Daniel told them was that his wife had seen an angel just before she died.

"Oh," Pauline said. "That must have been sad for him, but very hopeful too."

"I suppose," Doris said, picking up a sweet red pepper, turning it around in her hand, and then putting it back. Good grief!

"It just feels like so much has changed since that night, you know?"

Doris nodded and inched away from Pauline just enough to sort through the mound of wilting chives.

Much to Doris's dismay, Pauline was not to be so easily dismissed. "You can ask Daniel about it. He doesn't seem to mind talking about it," Doris said, holding up a disappointing bundle of chives. "In fact, since he told us, he has practically turned into some Holy Roller. Every answer for him is God. Like God can control anything real."

"Okay, thanks, I will. I work in the shop before class tomorrow, so that may give me a chance," Pauline said. "It just sounds so amazing. Did Daniel see the angel, too?"

"No," Doris said and turned the corner to the cracker aisle. How could a store mess up boxed crackers?

Finally, once she had shed Pauline, Doris got most of her shopping completed. She would have to take the extra time now to drive all the way to the other side of town to find decent produce. At least her chances of not running into anyone she would have to talk to would be better there.

Doris had just opened the back of her SUV to load her groceries when Phil Masters stopped by her car. "Can I help you with those?" Phil asked her.

Doris smiled a sweet dimply smile and thanked him.

She instantly remembered how Phil had the biggest crush on her in high school. Of course, most of the boys did, but Phil was always a little more suave than the standard roughnecks and farm boys. She had thought, before Frederick appeared and ruined her life, that she might just let herself be interested in Phil.

"Looks like you are stocking up for a long winter," Phil said, putting the last bag in her SUV and closing the back.

"Oh, it's just a little something I'm putting together for an art group I'm in."

"Yeah, I saw the signs," he said, standing in front of her now, just looking down into her face.

Doris's heart raced a little, and she could almost feel herself blushing like a schoolgirl. "Well, definitely stop by. I can't promise the art will impress, but I can promise you won't be disappointed in the presentation."

Phil nodded. "Maybe Sally and I will come. It sounds interesting."

Doris's smile dropped. That's right—Sally. Well, she would just see how things would go once every man in town found out she was finally getting a divorce from Frederick. It was never too late to start over, and this time she would be more selective. Phil said it was good to see her and went into the store. Doris got in behind the wheel and just sat there for a moment. She suddenly felt a little better. It was never too late to start her next future.

Doris decided to just drive the distance and get the rest of her shopping done before she went home. She cut through some residential streets as she knew this town inside and out. Doris was nearly down Canal Street when she frowned and slowed down. Was that Frederick's truck in front of that house? Of course, it was; how many identical trucks drove around with his company logo painted on the side? Doris didn't know whose house this was. She might know everyone, but she didn't follow them around to see where they lived! Doris circled the block and parked across the street a few houses down from the house under suspicion. She sat there gently chewing on the inside of her lip, a little upset, but not able to accept that what she saw was without a simple explanation.

Doris waited, and she waited. Well, actually, it was probably only a few minutes, but it, of course, felt eternal because of all the wild thoughts swirling in her imagination. Finally, the door opened, and Frederick came out first and then . . . then what? Was that his secretary? That was his secretary! Doris was sure of it. What was Frederick doing at his secretary's house other than the obvious! The obvious sucked the breath out of her body, and she sagged in on herself. Then to Doris's horror, she saw Frederick's secretary, whatever her name was—*Shirley,* she thought, *no, maybe Brenda*—anyway, that woman, that tot of a floozy, just reached up and hugged Doris's husband . . . right in front of Doris! The nerve!

Doris sat paralyzed with anger and hurt and mortification as that woman followed Frederick to his truck and talked to him for a few more eternities, then Frederick backed out of her driveway and was happily on his way. *His way to hell,* Doris screamed in her mind. Her hands shook as she put her SUV into drive and pulled out into the street. A car, she hadn't even thought to look for, was coming and blared its horn at her but, thank God, stopped just in time to avoid an accident. Now Doris was completely overwhelmed with fury. Frederick had almost gotten her killed! Oh, he was going to pay big-time now. This was way beyond anything he could ask forgiveness for. She would not be killed until she had wreaked havoc on his miserable cheating life!

Doris continued on to the produce store, sorting through her options of excruciating vengeance she could inflict on Frederick. She parked, looking for cross traffic before she pulled into the parking lot. She was not going to let Frederick injure her any further. She got out and slammed her door then lifted her chin and proceeded into the store. She selected a cart, pulled out her sanitizer and a Kleenex, and cleaned the hand bar, then headed straight for the tomatoes. Normally, she would not have to consult her list as she was that professional, but today was obviously not a normal day. She had to get this divorce behind her so she could be at peace with herself again.

Doris sorted and picked and opened packages to swap out bruises and weak color until she had the best she could do. She had seen pictures of the produce in Paris. She deserved that kind of perfection … at least in her food. Doris felt a sob in her chest and glanced around. No one was near her, but still she wouldn't weaken and let it out. Oh, it was so difficult being her.

By the time Frederick got home from work, Doris had the kitchen staged with her different food groupings. Concentrating on the success of her last big event before she had to pour all her energies and creativeness into punishing Frederick was what she had to focus on now. Certainly, after the embarrassing amount of compliments and praises she would receive on Wednesday evening, she would better be able to start the next torturous step she was forced to take. Doris stood at the counter with her back to Frederick.

"Wow. This is going to be some dinner tonight," Frederick said.

Doris knew he was joking, of course, which only made her hate him all the more. How could he think for one second that he could make light of this evening after he had been unfaithful right in front of her face!

"Want me to go out and pick something up for dinner?"

Really? Hadn't he picked up enough in one day? "I'm not hungry," Doris said, still not turning around. She couldn't bear to even look at him.

"How about wine? Can I get you some?"

"No, thanks. I can get whatever I need myself."

Doris could feel Frederick standing there, staring at her back, probably puzzled by her sudden chill. That was just how he had always taken her so for granted that he probably didn't know what to think when he came in one night and was finally treated the way he deserved.

Doris heard Frederick's footsteps coming toward her. She stiffened. Her shoulders ached from the stress of her day.

"What is it, Doris?"

"I have to concentrate, Frederick. There is so much to juggle right now."

"Can I help in any way?"

"I wish you could," she said and felt traitorous tears sting her eyes.

Doris felt Frederick's hands on her shoulders as he gently turned her to face him. "If this is too much for you, then we can hire someone to help you. All you need to do is tell me what you need."

Doris shook her head and backed away from him. "I can do it," she said. What she couldn't do was tolerate his fake tenderness. Fake or not, she was too vulnerable right now. She needed him, needed someone, to . . . see her—to appreciate her.

"Please, if you could just take care of yourself tonight. That is all I ask."

"Sure," Frederick said. "I can do that."

Doris nodded; she could feel her chin quiver, but she couldn't think about that now. She had to get back to work. Now that she had the food sorted, she needed to gather the serving dishes and her secret recipes.

Fran got up from her chair and clicked off the TV. For some reason her favorite shows were not as good as they used to be. Maybe they all changed the original writers to save money and were now trying to fool their loyal viewers, who knew how the characters should behave. She felt cheated by the writers and couldn't give them the satisfaction of thinking she was still watching their drivel.

Fran hobbled—her right knee was really giving her a fit lately— into the kitchen and turned on the light. She went to the sink to close the blinds and noticed that Eleanor and Trish were sitting on the front steps. They had jackets on, so it must be cold out. Why would they bring that tiny baby out into the cold night air? Trish probably didn't know better, but Eleanor should.

Fran closed the blinds and then hobbled to the hall closet to get her coat. She put it on. It had shrunk through the summer the way some clothes did that just hang in closets unused for long periods of time. Fran could barely zip it around her. Still, she was certain it would loosen up with a little wear.

When Fran stepped out on her porch, she could see why Eleanor and Trish were outside. The air was crisp, but the evening light was soft and quiet. It was best to get out and catch these perfect evenings before they were smothered by snow.

"Good evening," Fran called across the street as she dropped down in her swing.

Eleanor and Trish responded and then went back to talking— talking so quietly that Fran couldn't make it out no matter how hard she strained to hear. Finally, Fran was forced to get up and cross the street.

"Eleanor, do you know a good knee doctor?" Fran asked.

Eleanor said that she didn't. So far, thank goodness, she hadn't had any problems with her knees.

"Well," Fran said, "we will see if that changes when you have to get down in the dirt to plant your garden come spring."

"We'll see," Eleanor said.

"Are you going to keep up with Bill's garden? He put a lot into getting the soil built up for a good garden. It would be a shame to let it go."

"If Mom wants a garden, I will be here to help," Trish said.

"So," Fran said, "you think you'll stay through the winter? Bet you've forgotten how miserable winter can be, what with you living in Florida all these years."

"Oh, one never forgets what winter is like."

"But you are staying anyway?"

"We are," Trish said.

"Humph," Fran said. "So I guess you will be looking for a job, then. Good luck in this town."

"Thanks," Trish said as though she thought Fran really meant the part about good luck.

"We don't have any limousine services here. What are you going to do?"

"Who knows, maybe I'll start one," Trish said, and Fran knew she was just being flippant.

"Guess that means you'll be saddling your mother with raising another kid. And at her age."

Eleanor assured Fran that however things worked out, she would be happy with it.

"What about your painting classes and going to church?" Fran asked Eleanor. "You giving all that up?"

"The painting classes are over tomorrow, but yes, I think it is time I started going to church. I honestly don't know why I haven't."

"Which one are you planning to go to?" Fran asked.

"Well, Bill's funeral was at the Methodist church, so I think that is where I will go. The minister was so gracious when we weren't even members."

"Methodist, heh?" Fran repeated.

"Yes."

"Do you mind if I ride along with you next Sunday?" Fran was surprised herself by the question. She hadn't thought of going back to church. Where did that come from?

"Of course," Eleanor said.

"Now I'm not interested in taking any Bible study classes or getting involved, really. I just want to go and see what I get."

"Certainly," Eleanor agreed. "I'll be leaving at eight thirty."

"Fine," Fran said. "Fine." And then she turned and hobbled back across the street. She had better get home before she agreed to something else she hadn't intended to get involved with.

When Fran had left, Trish turned to her mother. "When did this happen—you wanting to go to church?"

Eleanor looked past Trish and frowned a little. "Something happened in my painting class a few days ago, and I haven't been able to stop thinking about it."

"What?"

Eleanor explained about Elizabeth and Daniel's wife's dying words. "I've wondered if your dad was escorted by an angel. I hope he was. He was a good man."

Trish cuddled her daughter a little tighter. "Maybe we will go with you Sunday," Trish said, then she laughed. "Holy crap, I'm home a couple of days, and now I'm going to church, and I'm going with my mother and Fran."

Eleanor smiled at Trish and knew they would be okay. Why, who knew, maybe the next big thing would be seeing Trish remove that disturbing eyebrow stud.

"Burr," Trish said. "Let's go in. Once the sun sets, it's freezing. Hey, can we start a fire? I think I actually missed sitting in front of the fireplace and talking."

"Trish, you never sat quietly in front of the fireplace, and you never had fireside conversations with us."

Trish laughed. "Yeah, that's probably why I thought I missed it. Somewhere in my mind I thought it would be nice. Of course, that was probably in September when I was about sick of the humidity and heat of Florida."

"Well, come February, I hope you don't start dreaming about the humidity and heat."

Trish looked down at her sleeping baby. "I think I'm over running. I really want to grow up now. It's funny that this tiny, little being came along and changed everything. I can't think only about myself any longer. You know, Mom, I worry that the pain of childbirth wasn't really the hard part."

"As long as there is hope of a prodigal-son moment, the struggles and disappointments will all be worth it," Eleanor said. Trish looked confused, but Eleanor just smiled and got up to get an arm load of firewood from the shed.

Tuesday's class was quiet, each woman working to get their last painting as perfect as they could and trying not to think ahead of the critiques—trying not to think of the unkindness these townspeople were capable of, gossiping snide things behind your back and then stopping in front of you to smile and compliment you. Whose stupid idea was this anyway?

Finally, Elizabeth broke the silence. "I'm terrified."

All the others mumbled agreement.

"Well, it seemed like a good idea at the time," Doris said, defending herself as the one who decided at the beginning of their apprenticeship that, of course, they would all produce great art under Daniel's guidance. And of course, she would then be able to upstage them all with her additional entertaining talents. She had, apparently, greatly underestimated herself and everyone else. What was the saying about a swine's ear?

"Ladies," Daniel said, walking among them, "trust me. You all have put the best of yourselves on your canvases. And I know you will be surprised with the enthusiastic responses you'll receive tomorrow."

"We love you, Daniel," Ruthie said. "We do, but stumbling along week after week here in our safe little space was one thing. Now we have to let the world in."

Daniel laughed. "The world will wish they had been a part of what you women have accomplished."

The women looked from Daniel to around the room at one another—a ragtag collection of vastly different women who, until this painting class, would never even have noticed one another on the street. Now, though they never dreamed they would feel this way, they actually felt a little sad that this struggle of trying to paint, this struggle of tolerating one another, was over. *Over.* They would clean their painting supplies, pack them neatly into their cases, and then walk away.

Pauline just had to ask. "Daniel, can't you start another class?" But he had said, sadly, that his lease was nearly up on the shop, and he thought it was time for him to go back to Boston.

"Do you remember," he asked, "the first class when everyone was afraid to even make that first paint stroke on the canvas? Now look at you."

They all paused and remembered too. Then Eleanor said that they had certainly come a long way, but they wouldn't have been able to do any of it without him. Everyone nodded.

"Well, thanks," he said. "But in all honesty, I will admit that anything I may have done to help you has also helped me. I came wounded, and because of all of you, I am at a better place. It seems God gives us what we need whether we ask for it or not."

Everyone teared a little. Carolyn actually sniffled, and everyone looked at her. "I'm sorry. I've just been so emotional lately."

"Hey," Daniel said, "why don't we all take a break? I brought snacks and beverages. Let's go in the back, assume our usual crates, and go over Doris's plans for tomorrow. We can relax a little and then finish up these last paintings."

Doris, Eleanor, and Ruthie were delighted to see wine as a beverage, but Elizabeth and Pauline settled for the ginger ale, and Carolyn declined anything. Aside from her emotional sensitivity, Carolyn was just teetering on the verge of nausea lately.

"Then eat a few crackers," Pauline advised. "When I was pregnant with my twins the first few months, I was nauseous every day. Then I found that if I ate a little something every couple of hours, I would feel better."

Carolyn looked surprised. Pregnant? She couldn't possibly, after all these years of monthly failures, be pregnant?

"Oh, I'm not suggesting that you are pregnant. I'm just saying that eating a little bit when you feel nauseous may help. A couple of crackers. Some ginger ale. That's all."

Carolyn nodded. Even the sudden thought of eating made her feel emotional. Pregnant? Had she missed her cycle? She grabbed a Ritz cracker.

Doris retrieved her notebook and her glass of chardonnay and stepped into the middle of the circle. "I am proud to report that I have badgered Daniel into showing some of his work. After all, we are inviting the whole town to come, we actually need something worthy for them to see."

The women laughed at the truth of that.

"I will need you all to come an hour early to arrange your paintings how you would like to show them. Daniel and I have laid out the floor plan of who will be where and where the food and beverage tables will be. I'm afraid my food and decoration plans may be a little over the top, but as they say, too much of a good thing is a good thing. So I will pass this around now so you will have an idea of where you will be when you come in tomorrow."

Doris handed her notebook to Eleanor and stepped to get a nibble while the women looked at her plan. Daniel had done a decent job of buying pre-made platters of meats, cheeses, and fruits. She smiled to herself. Just wait until they see what a professional can put out. Doris was feeling better tonight than she had since she had witnessed Frederick's affair with his secretary. She had pretended being distracted by this event so Frederick would leave her alone. She certainly did not have the strength, with all this, to deal with confronting him before he was served the divorce papers. She had called her attorney after her discovery of his infidelity to add that devastating crime to the divorce papers. She wanted it right there in black and white for Frederick to have to answer to. Doris took a large drink of her wine. She needed to get refocused. She shook Frederick from her mind and turned to the women.

"Any questions now that you have seen the plan?" she asked.

"Well," Ruthie said, "one. What are you all wearing? I mean this looks so fancy."

"We are presenting ourselves as artists," Doris said. "So I suppose we can be as diverse as our paintings. All within good taste, of course."

"It's just that Max bought me two dresses—who would have dreamed, right? And well, anyway, now I don't even know which one to wear. So I thought I'd check with all of you, and maybe that would help me."

Elizabeth said she had decided on black slacks and a white blouse. Eleanor said she had a suit; it was old, but it still fit and matched the autumn colors in her first painting. Carolyn said she had a white flowery embroidered blouse she was going to wear with a floor-length denim shirt. Pauline said she had a cobalt-blue dress with matching shoes that she had bought for a wedding. And Doris said she had ordered an embellished lace sheath dress from her favorite store in New York that fit her like it was made specifically for her. It was actually a bronzy goldish color under beige lace. The sheath part had a sheen to it, so it was gorgeous under the lace. Fortunately, she already had ordered shoes a couple of months ago that she didn't actually have anything to wear them with, but now she did. So after she bought herself the perfect jewelry tomorrow, she would be set. Ah yes, Frederick, you worm, you are buying your faithful, loyal wife new and expensive jewelry.

Ruthie thought of all their choices. They made it sound so obvious and simple. Why was it so hard for her to decide? Max had known her deficiency in following through on important things, so he had taken care of it. When Ruthie had come home from the diner to rest and change her clothes, she found two dresses hanging on the closet door. What a guy! Max certainly had his faults, but once in a blue moon, he'd sneak in something that really caught Ruthie off guard—dresses. She honestly couldn't even imagine the sight of Max in a dress shop, picking through the racks. He had done a good job though. Of course, the poor store clerk had probably helped with the final choices, but still they were her size and something she might have bought herself if she had gotten to the store.

"Thanks," Ruthie said to the women. "That helps."

Daniel sat listening to the women. God certainly worked in mysterious ways. Daniel realized now that each woman in his class had been chosen for a reason. He had seen the raw need in Pauline and Eleanor. He had been, quite frankly, surprised by Elizabeth and Doris wanting to join the class, but now he saw it had been right. Carolyn was looking for something to fill her emptiness, and Ruthie . . . Ruthie was an artist despite herself. He didn't know Ruthie's story, but her paintings spoke of the dreams inside her. Daniel hoped they all realized God's touch in their lives.

Break and the wine were finished, and everyone moved back into the front of the store to finish their canvases.

"If any of you are interested in selling any of your paintings," Daniel said, "it would not be wrong to have a price posted by the painting."

"Selling?" Doris snorted. "I couldn't afford what it would cost me to get someone to even take one of my paintings."

"Yeah," Ruthie said. "I'd first have to have a description so people would even know what it was supposed to be."

"Maybe you could help us," Elizabeth said. "We don't have a clue what to put. I mean just in case someone may actually want one of our paintings."

"First," Daniel said, "you have to understand that the clientele in Gilmont is not the same as in Boston. You are also novice artists. Though there is real talent evident here, I still think we should not get our expectations set too high. So if you would like to sell them— you can, of course, keep your work—then I will do the best I can to help you price them."

"Don't even bother with me," Doris said.

"I'd be interested," Pauline said. "I actually have three more that I have finished at home that I'd like to bring tomorrow."

"I think I want to keep mine," Carolyn said.

Ruthie said she didn't have any room for paintings in her life, so if she could sell them, she would be happy.

And Eleanor said she was pleased to just show her paintings. Their worth to her was just in the doing of them.

Daniel helped those who wanted to sell and then took all the women into the back to show them frames they might want to purchase. "Your selling price would then include the cost of the frame," he said.

Decisions were made, and the evening was over. Daniel watched as each woman left his shop. He had not intended to give classes. He had come to Gilmont on a whim. He'd felt the need to just make a change, to take a break from the absence of Jill. Of course, that absence was in his heart, not just the rooms of their apartment or the shop they owned together or the streets they walked. His love for Jill would be wherever he went, so he might as well stop trying to run from it and just go home.

⸻∿∘⚬⟨⚬⟩⚬∘∿⸻

On Wednesday morning Frederick walked into the kitchen to find Doris busy at work. There were cutting boards and pots and recipes taped on cupboard doors. She had soft rock playing, and she hummed to Air Supply's "All Out of Love" as she flittered around the room, checking to be certain the ingredients for each item were under the recipe taped to the cabinet. The churchwomen would be here soon, and she needed to have everything organized so all they had to do was follow directions.

Her heart was happy until . . . she saw unfaithful, heartless Frederick, and then she turned her back to the sight of him and tried to refocus—crab stuffing. Yes, she needed to get the celery seeds for that.

"Do you think you will be back to yourself when this is all over?" unfaithful, heartless Frederick asked.

Doris ignored his rude question and moved on to the liver pâté recipe. She was certain she had bought enough cream for that and the whipped topping for the tarts. She had better check now before the cooking started. Doris walked around Frederick to get to the refrigerator.

"Well?" unfaithful, heartless Frederick persisted.

"Can't you see that my mind is stretched to a million things? Now is not a good time to harass me."

"For God's sake, Doris, I'm not trying to harass you. I'm trying to understand what is happening to you."

Doris glanced at the clock. She had forty-five minutes until the women came. She was not certain if that was enough time to have a major fight with Frederick and then still have time to repair her nerves and makeup before the women came.

"There are things you and I need to talk about," Doris said. "But they will just have to wait until tomorrow."

"Fine. So glad you can finally fit me in," Frederick snapped and then turned and left the kitchen.

Doris tried to shake it off. He was wrong. She was right. That was the bottom line. He did not have the moral right to question her behavior about anything. Who did he think he was anyway? Did he think she was stupid and didn't know about him and his little tart? If it was only one little tart. What if Frederick had several? What if he had been unfaithful their whole marriage? Doris's knees felt weak. Now was not the time for her to torture herself with these thoughts. She had to focus on the greatest gala event this town had ever witnessed. She had to impress and shine as she had never done before.

Doris glanced around the kitchen and then remembered she had left her notebook on her chaise lounge. She headed for the stairs just as the door closed behind Frederick. Good. He was out of her sight. Doris went into her room to retrieve her notebook when she noticed a gift box on top of the notebook. Doris frowned and picked it up, suspicious of it. She untied the ribbon and unwrapped the box. *How dare he?* She opened the box with the jeweler's name written in gold letters. Inside was a bronzy goldish necklace with tiny diamonds sparkling in a V shape in the middle. Doris stared at it as though it were some foreign Kryptonite object from outer space. What? How could Frederick have known? Doris sank down on the chaise lounge. Her shoulders sagged under the unbelievable audacity of her husband. She could not be bought with jewelry, but still . . . no. She could not forgive him just because he bought her the perfect, most beautiful necklace that perfectly matched her perfect outfit for tonight.

Doris snapped close the lid of the box. She couldn't look at it any longer. The big question was, of course, how could Frederick have known about her clothes for tonight? He never knew what she was wearing when he was looking right at her. She would swear on her son's life that she could be standing there talking to Frederick and then suddenly spin him around and ask him what she was wearing, and he wouldn't have a clue. Now, he knew about her new outfit? Did he have people at the post office reporting to him about her deliveries? Was he monitoring her charges and knew she had ordered her outfit online and traced it from there? How did he know?

Doris got up to get a tissue from the bathroom, and when she walked past her closet, she saw the new outfit hanging there right in plain view. Okay. Okay, so it was open and obvious, and he might have seen it when he had come out of his own closet . . . but even so, what made that selfish wart think of going out and getting her a beautiful necklace to match it?

Ah, of course, he had taken a photo of her outfit on his cell phone and taken it into work and probably sent that twit of a tot out to find something to match. They were probably scheming together to keep the little wife distracted and happy. Doris narrowed her eyes at the sudden thought that maybe, just maybe, Frederick had told the tot to get herself something nice while she was at it.

Doris could hardly breathe through her anger. What had she ever done to deserve such heartless treatment? Who could have had a more devoted and faithful wife than Frederick? Oh, how she hated him.

Doris stumbled back to her chaise lounge and dropped the necklace box on the floor beside her. She stretched out and closed her eyes. She had to pull herself together before the churchwomen came. She had to focus on tonight—just get through tonight, and all hell would break loose for Frederick. A tear squeezed out, and she cursed him as she wiped it away.

⁓∽○⌇○⌇○∽⁓

The doors of the Rotary Club opened at five o'clock, and all was ready. What a day—women in and out with food, paintings being hung or set on easels, and lights swaying from the ceiling or positioned on the floor, either pointing directly at the canvas or filtering the light to soften the painting. Name tags had been made, soft music was playing ever so quietly in the background, and words were hushed to near whispers. Hearts were excited and afraid.

Daniel walked around like a proud father encouraging each woman, giving them confidence . . . until he left them and walked on to the next. Even Doris, who had commanded the whole day like an army general—so detailed were her instructions that no one dared to deviate—now stood by her paintings as uncertain as the rest of the women about what was going to happen when people actually came in ... if anyone actually came in.

And then slowly, slowly, they began to trickle in. Daniel stood by the door, welcoming each guest and inviting them to enjoy the art and, please, stop by the food tables. He was certain no one would leave disappointed.

Daniel met Tim and the twins first. Tim had left work early to get the family ready for the big evening. Pauline's family had apparently been waiting outside the door for it to open.

"Really, I can't thank you enough for helping Pauline take these classes," Tim said. "I guess I never understood how important this was to her."

"She has a gifted eye for color. I hope she continues," Daniel said. "In fact, if we get a chance later, I would like to talk to you and Pauline about her running the shop for the remaining three months of my lease. I'm ready to get back to my gallery in Boston."

Tim looked troubled by the prospect.

"It's just an offer," Daniel continued. "Of course, I would pay her, and she could continue to paint at the shop when things were slow."

"You think she is good, then?" Tim asked.

"Oh yes. If her work doesn't sell tonight, in this market, then I'd like to take it back to my gallery and see how it does."

"Whoa," Tim said.

Daniel smiled at his surprise. "You haven't seen any of her work?"

"No, she has done a great job of keeping it a secret. I'm pretty stoked to see it now though."

"Well, prepare to be impressed," Daniel said, "and to be as surprised as Pauline was when she finished her first painting."

Next came Elizabeth's parents and grandmother. Samuel greeted Daniel and thanked him for being there when Twilight broke out of her cocoon.

Daniel nodded. "I don't know where she will go from here, but I hope she keeps painting. I have never seen anyone put so much emotion on the canvas. She reaches deep, and it shows."

Elizabeth's grandmother reached her hand out to take Daniel's. "God sent you for that girl. I know it."

"Well," Daniel said, wrapping both his strong hands around hers, "I would like to think I was an instrument sent by God, but really, I started this as just a wounded soldier myself."

"Aren't we all?" Gram said. "Aren't we all?"

Next came Carolyn's husband. Charlie was dressed in pressed slacks, a white button-down shirt, and a green tie. His shaggy blond hair was still damp from his shower and pushed behind his ears. He looked Daniel in the eye and thanked him.

"Carolyn said she is really going to miss these classes," Charlie said. "She sort of stunned me when she said she wanted to take them. I never thought she wanted to paint, you know." Charlie shrugged and shook his head like he still was confused by it.

"The detail in her work is very impressive," Daniel said.

"Really? Yeah, I guess I can see that," Charlie said. "She puts a lot into everything she does, except for herself. This is the first thing she has ever done just for herself. Guess that's what surprised me when I realized it."

"You are lucky to have her," Daniel said, and Charlie agreed and moved on to go see his wife on her big night.

A steady stream of curious townspeople came in, pleased to be greeted by Daniel and pleased he had brought something like this to their town. Several cliques of high-school students came in and, in their youthful insecurity, avoided Daniel in case he might expect them to know anything in particular about art and, instead, visited the food tables and wandered among the paintings to see what the fuss was about.

Elizabeth's parents and grandmother came across the room, smiling at her. Elizabeth was grateful to see them, grateful her family was there.

"My goodness," her grandmother said, seeing Elizabeth's painting for the first time. "You had a lot on your mind when you painted these."

"You have no idea," Elizabeth said.

Elizabeth's mother teared up. Thankfully, she had a hankie wadded in her hand just in case, and she now dabbed at her eyes. "Your dad tried to prepare me for these, but still they are a little overwhelming."

"I don't think I will be painting like this anymore," Elizabeth said. "I guess I just had to get it all out of my system. But Daniel did say he thought my paintings were good—for what they are, I mean."

"Oh, Sweetie, they are great. I mean, the detail and all," her mother said. "And your father was right, these do show us that you are really out of that dark, lonely place you had been in. I'm so happy."

Elizabeth's father looked at the painting now that had not been corrected when he had seen them. The emotion on his face spoke of what he could not say.

"I see you are wanting to sell them," Gram said. "And I think I will just buy one. No, two. Heck," she said, waving her old hand in the air, "I'll take all three."

Elizabeth laughed. "Gram, you don't have to buy them. You can have them if you really want them. I just didn't know what else to do with them because I know I will paint differently from now on."

"Nope," Gram said, "I want to pay you for them. You did the work, you deserve the money. And besides, these are special. These are proof that you were touched by God. My little granddaughter was touched by God!"

Elizabeth blushed and shrugged. "More like winked at than touched," she said.

Elizabeth's dad reached up and peeled the price stickers off the wall beside the paintings. "These need to stay in the family. We need to put them in the dining room so we can see them every Sunday when we sit down for dinner together." And then he added, "After we come home from church."

Elizabeth was about to break down and actually hug her father in public when the four dark souls that had been skirting the room stopped at her area to look at her paintings. She was a little embarrassed for her peers to see her work. She had pretty much envisioned this evening consisting of artsy elderly people who had the leisure to make this extra effort on a Wednesday evening. But here they were, studying the painting, obviously confused and betrayed by the whiteness that disguised the truth of the painting. They stood working to pull out the despair of the darkness under the angel's touch.

One girl, whose black ringed eyes darted from the painting to Elizabeth and back to the painting again as she chewed at her ragged thumbnail, appeared to want to ask something, but when the others moved on, she went with them. Elizabeth watched her, hoping the girl would see her interest and come back and ask her question.

Brandon and Cathy, who had invited her into their church group, appeared next and nodded at Elizabeth's work, obviously getting what she had done.

"Who is the little boy?" Brandon asked.

"He was my uncle," Elizabeth said. And then because her family had moved on to see the other paintings, she felt she could ask them something that had been troubling her. "Do you believe," she said, "that babies, tiny babies who had never had a chance to know about Jesus, get to go to heaven if they die?"

Brandon and Cathy nodded. "Most definitely," Brandon said. "Jesus said, 'Let the little children come to me and do not hinder them, for such belongs the kingdom of heaven.'"

"Thank you," Elizabeth said, so relieved that her unborn brothers and sisters were in heaven. "And it's pretty impressive that you can quote Jesus."

"Oh," Cathy said. "Brandon's dad is the minister of our church. Plus Brandon wants to go to seminary after we graduate. Yeah, he knows scripture."

Elizabeth knew then that she definitely needed to be a part of what they had. She needed to know the answers to such questions as her uncle's and siblings' eternity, and selfishly, she wanted that contented charity and peace that Brandon and Cathy seemed to have. Even though she had been so dark for so long, they had never reproached her, and even then, at the first sign of her shedding that part of her life, they had come to her and invited her in.

"You're good," Brandon said, studying her painting. "Keep working on the angels. The more you know them, the more they will light up your art."

"Thanks," Elizabeth said. "I will."

Brandon and Cathy moved on, and Elizabeth glanced around to see where her parents were when she noticed the dark-eyed girl watching her. The girl was close enough to have heard her conversation with Brandon. Elizabeth smiled at her and knew that however long it took, that girl would approach her one day, and Elizabeth would help coax her out of the darkness.

Eleanor was standing by her paintings, talking to one of the women who helped set up the food today. She knew the woman was from Doris's church, so she flinched a little when Trish came in with Ella in her arms. *So it begins,* Eleanor thought, *the judging and the gossip.* It was not that anyone else's opinions of Trish's morals would, for one instant, intimidate Trish; in fact, Eleanor pitied anyone who even tried to question Trish about her choices, but still Eleanor wished she could protect Trish and Ella from any unpleasantness.

"Hey, Mom," Trish said. "This is some fancy affair you have here."

"Yes," Eleanor said. "Doris really outdid herself." Then Eleanor introduced Trish and Ella to the woman.

"I just had to stop and talk to your mother," the lady said. "I was looking at her paintings today when we were setting up, and they just make me feel so comforted somehow. Like they are telling me I should stop all the rushing and doing and just stroll down a beautiful path in the woods." The woman sighed. "What's happened to us?"

"Madness," Trish said. "It's sheer madness, what we do to ourselves."

The woman laughed. "Well, enjoy your precious little bundle, and don't forget to take her for strolls down beautiful paths."

"I'm on it," Trish said.

The woman smiled sweetly at them and moved on. Trish stepped back and looked at her mother's work.

"I didn't know what to expect," Trish said. "As far as I ever knew, your talents were limited to panda-bear birthday cakes and Halloween costumes. But, Mom, these are pretty good."

"Thanks."

"What did Dad think? Did he see any of these?"

Eleanor shook her head. "He really didn't understand why I wanted to do this. I suppose I didn't understand it enough myself to explain it to him. So we just didn't talk about it. I wish now that I had shown him. He might have liked them."

"I don't know," Trish said. "You would have had to add a deer hanging from one of those trees or paint a garden tractor chugging down the road for him to really like them."

Eleanor smiled at the truth of that. Her Bill had been a simple man. He had appreciated hard work, and that was about it. She did wish he could have been here tonight though. He would have come to support her, to be here in case no one else came, but then she was certain, he would have seen that her painting had been something necessary, something Eleanor had needed to do while she was waiting for Trish to come home. Bill would have finally understood. Eleanor reached out and took Ella. She cradled her close and accepted that grief had caught up with her. Thank God, she had her girls to help her through.

For a few precious hours, Doris would allow herself to revel in her glory, for every detail was just as she had envisioned it. Every food item was tasty and artfully arranged. Her beverage station was sparkling with colorful carafes of assorted beverages and bowls of ice. The lighting and streamers were sophisticatedly understated. And her dress! Her dress was even more perfect than she had imagined, and then to add the crowning jewel because she couldn't help but appreciate the envy it would evoke and because no one would have to know the sordid circumstance of its procurement, she even wore Frederick's necklace. She had tried every other piece of jewelry she owned, and nothing else was even close to being suitable. So she had finally, tearfully, decided that it was perfect no matter what sewer it had come from. Besides, Frederick would never show his face at an art exhibit, so he would never know she had even worn it.

Doris had left her paintings to speak for themselves, and she desperately hoped they would remain mute in the far corner as she went fluttering throughout the room, looking as though she was not conscious in the least of all the fuss being made over her spectacular success when . . . what? Was that really Frederick's secretary coming right at her, walking with an innocent smile on her face as though she was not afraid of what Doris might do to it?

"I just had to find you," stupid Brenda or Sophie or whoever it was dared to say.

"Really?" Even Doris doubted anyone could evoke such ice with one word.

"Yes, I just had to tell you what a wonderful husband you have."

Doris was speechless—literally speechless.

"He may not have told you, he is probably not one to brag about his generosity, and so you may not know how truly generous he is, but I honestly don't know what I would have done if Frederick . . ."

Frederick? She dared to say his name? Doris had stopped listening. Her mind was racing in a thousand directions. Should she just give in to it and tackle the little wench right here in the middle of the room and beat her down? Or should she retain her dignity and walk away to, perhaps, the biggest goon in the room to order him to escort that brainless tart out before Doris was forced to erupt and cause the scene of all scenes? I mean, the nerve! And right here in the middle of Doris's brilliant gala!

"Anyway," the tart continued, obviously oblivious to the full threat of Doris, "when I told him how my husband had lost his job and had to go to South Carolina to work for his father and how now I discovered that there was a water leak rotting out my floor in the bathroom, and of course, rot is not covered in your homeowner's insurance—who knew, right? Anyway, when I told Frederick I couldn't sell the house with rot, and right now we didn't have the money to repair it, well, he came to my house to inspect it and . . ." Now really, there were tears glistening in the near-adolescent's eyes, like Doris had sympathy for fake tears.

"And he is going to send his guys over to repair the damage for free." The little twit nodded her tot face and sniffed.

"And just why would he do that?" Doris heard herself ask.

"Because he is a wonderful man. I've seen him help many people but never dreamed I would need him to do anything for me. So I know he wouldn't think of letting me repay him, but I wanted you to know that Jack and I will repay whatever it costs. We'll send the money as soon as we get set up in South Carolina. Really, we will."

Doris paused in her fury. Could this be true? Could Frederick have only gone to this child's house to inspect rot damage? Did he do random, generous things for people?

"What do you think of my necklace?" Doris asked and watched the tot's face as she answered. No one could fool Doris with fake responses.

The little twit smiled innocently at Doris's necklace. "It's beautiful."

"Have you ever seen this necklace before?"

The girl frowned and shook her head. "No. I'd remember one like that. Is it like one worn by someone famous?"

Doris was done with her. "Never mind," she said and started to walk past Frederick's little secretary.

"I just wanted you to know that we are grateful and will repay—"

"Whatever," Doris said. "If Frederick wants to fix your rot, that is up to him." Doris put her hand to her throat and walked back to the corner where her horrible art awaited her. She had to think. She had to calm down and think about what had just happened. Had Frederick actually picked out this necklace? Had he spent his time trying to find the perfect necklace to match her dress? Doris shook her head. *Frederick?*

"Well, whom do I see about purchasing these paintings?"

Doris heard Frederick's voice and whirled around. There he was, grinning and handsome and so full of himself. Her heart prickled to life a little.

"Why are there no prices on these paintings?" he demanded to know.

Doris looked at him like he was crazy. "Because I didn't want to embarrass myself," she said.

"What? I love 'em."

"Shhh, lower your voice."

"Then tell me how much you want for them. All three of them. I've gotta have them all."

"Please, Frederick, stop being so ridiculous."

"A thousand? Will you sell them for a thousand?"

"I'm not selling them for a dollar, okay? I know they are not any good, and I'm not going to be anyone's charity case."

Frederick stepped close to her—very close. "Look, Sweetheart, these are great. They are the first things I've seen from you in years that are just basic and honest and humble. They show that somewhere in this outrageous, obsessive, domineering woman, there is a tender spot of vulnerability. I love them."

Doris opened her mouth to protest then closed it. "Really?" she said. "You want them?"

"Yeah," he said and gave her that look, the one with one devilish eyebrow raised and a smirk on his lips that she could never resist. She hated him, but she couldn't resist that look.

"Did you pick out this necklace yourself?" She had to know.

"Who else have you been showing your new dress to?"

"And the chaise lounge? Why did you buy that?"

"Because you asked for it?"

"Yes, but you never get things I ask for. I have to get them and pretend they are from you."

"No, you have never had to do that. You just did that. I may be slow, but I do want to give you the things that make you happy."

"Sure. Everything, maybe, but what I really want."

"Well then, let's blow this joint, and I'll see what I can do."

Doris pushed him away and giggled like a schoolgirl.

"I've been thinking about a cruise," Frederick said. "You know, like the one in the booklet you left on my desk. What do you say? A cruise? Just you and me?"

"I don't know," Doris said. "I was thinking of Paris."

Frederick laughed. "You're impossible. I'll give you a week in Paris for the paintings and not a day longer."

Ruthie stood rigid beside her paintings of whatever they were. She could see people pausing to look at them—studying them, really, probably trying to figure them out. One woman sent her husband close enough to see the prices attached to them. But then they moved on. She didn't care, really, if they sold or not. She lived without the money before she painted them, and she would live if she never sold them. What she might not live through, she admitted, was if her girls chose not to come.

Max had bought himself a new shirt for the art show. He stood behind Ruthie now in a crisp pressed cotton shirt that was dark blue with thin pinstripes. The sleeves were rolled up a cuff or two as he told her if he had to iron his own shirt for her big shindig, then he was going to wear it the way he wanted. She had told him to wear it on his butt if he wanted to. Max had even gotten a haircut today. He didn't wear it long enough for one of those biker ponytails, but it could get a little shaggy at times before he noticed it.

Ruthie glanced at him once in a while to make herself feel a little better. Max had offered, on one of his trips to the food tables, to get her something, a chocolate-and-raspberry-mousse tart, maybe— he knew she loved chocolate—or maybe a glass of something? But she just couldn't. "You go ahead, God knows you won't get a chance to eat anything like this stuff again," she had said, glancing at the clock and then the door.

"Excuse me," the woman who had sent her husband up to check the paintings' prices said.

Ruthie pulled her mind back to the art show.

"We were wondering if you could ... if you needed to get that exact price for this painting or if there was room to discuss it," she said.

"Oh, I didn't pick these prices, Daniel did. It's pretty much a guesstimate, you could say."

"So you may take less? I'm not saying that the paintings aren't worth what you are asking, it's just that, well, we don't ever buy art, real art, so we don't have extra money for that kind of thing. But I just can't stop looking at this one." She pointed to one that had a castle on a hill and then three figures, three girls, in the meadow below.

"Sold," said Ruthie.

"But we haven't even talked about the price."

"How much are you wanting to pay?"

The woman looked a little flustered. She glanced at her husband, who was standing at a safe distance so he wouldn't have to appear to be a part of his wife's embarrassing price haggling. He wasn't sold on that painting anyway. It was a little too blurry for him. Why, he bet his wife could paint one like that herself if she wanted to.

"You give me half what the sticker says, and it is yours," Ruthie finally said.

"Half? Really? That's great. Thanks. Thank you, I really do love it." Then the woman motioned for her husband to come over and give Ruthie the money.

"No. I'm afraid you'll have to pick it up and pay for it tomorrow at Daniel's shop. We are keeping them to show until eight when we close down," Ruthie said. "But I'll write your name and the price on this sticker and put it on the back so Daniel will know what we agreed to."

The transaction was verbally completed, and the couple moved on.

"Remind me to never ever let you sell anything of mine," Max said.

"Shut up, Max," Ruthie hissed at him.

"Hey, look, is that them?" Max asked. "Must be because the smaller one looks just like you."

Ruthie's heart froze. Her whole body froze. She actually could not even turn around and look at the door.

"Are they coming over here?" Ruthie whispered.

"Yes," Max whispered back.

"Oh god," Ruthie said.

"Pretend you are brave," Max whispered.

Ruthie glared at him and then took a deep breath and turned around, a forced smile already plastered on her face. She was glad she had worn the coral dress Max had bought. It was a simple wraparound that tied at the side, but that color on her, along with her big jewelry pieces, made her look a little like herself, only maybe a little better. Ruthie smoothed the front of her skirt and started walking toward the girls.

The three met in the center of the room. The girls seemed as nervous as Ruthie.

"Thank you" was all that Ruthie could get out.

Her girls were thirteen and fourteen now. And Max was right; Juliet did favor Ruthie in appearance, but when Natasha started talking, taking charge with a cockiness that set the tone, Ruthie knew who was giving their father the biggest problems.

"This is really nice," Juliet said, looking around at the whole room. "We didn't know you even painted."

"We still don't," Natasha said. "Where's yours?"

"Over here," Ruthie said, pointing and leading them to her space. "They aren't anything to brag about," she began so they would know she was aware that they were not that good.

"Oh, impressionism!" Juliet said. "I love impressionism."

Ruthie looked at her paintings. "There is a name for this?"

"Yeah," Natasha said. "Our bookworm. She either knows a lot or pretends to, and we are too stupid to know if she is right or not."

Juliet frowned at her sister. "I'm not the one who lies about stuff."

Natasha shrugged. "Telling people what they want to hear is a way of protecting them. I'm just very considerate like that. That's all."

"Girls," Robert said, walking between them and slipping his arms around their shoulders. "We talked about this." He smiled at Ruthie. "You know, at times I thought I might miss your feistiness, but nope, I still live with it."

"But not me," Juliet protested.

"No, Juliet, not you."

Natasha wiggled out from his arm. "Please. Give me a break."

"You know," Ruthie said, "if I'd had a father who gave me a tenth of what your father has given you two, I bet I wouldn't have back talked him."

"Oh, I don't," Juliet said. "I never do."

"And what about your mother?" Natasha asked. "What did she ever give you?"

Ruthie looked right at Natasha. "Life," she said.

Max controlled his urge to high-five Ruthie. Yup, he was proposing to that woman tonight.

"And what if you wanted more?" Natasha asked, looking right back at Ruthie.

"Then I would ask for it and give her the chance to make it right."

Juliet stepped forward and wrapped her thin arms around her mother. "I missed you," Juliet said.

Ruthie closed her eyes and hugged her daughter back.

"Okay," Natasha said after the dramatic hugging had finally broken. "I want more."

Ruthie knew better than to try and hug Natasha, but her soaring heart wanted to. It wanted to squeeze her so tight Natasha wouldn't remember a time she had been without her mother.

"And so let's do it," Ruthie said. Then she looked at Robert, hoping she hadn't overstepped the lines of their agreement.

"Happy to share," he said.

Finally, Linda came up behind them with her and Robert's son. The little boy was about three and so cute Ruthie wanted to hug him too. Seriously, what had just happened? Who had turned the light switch on in her life?

Finally, the big night drew to a close. The churchwomen had made the food and dishes magically disappear, the lighting crew had rolled extension cords and put away their ladders, and the paintings had been sorted—any sold were going to the shop with Daniel, and all others were going home with their artists.

Daniel and the women, with their families, stood by the door, the empty hall now just a memory of the drama and glory of this evening.

"Doris, you did an amazing job. We all thank you," Daniel said.

Doris beamed. "I even sold all my paintings."

"You did?" Ruthie asked and then added that, of course, she did; they were great.

"Well, yes, I did if one can count one's husband as a legitimate buyer."

"Best deal I ever made," Frederick said, slipping his arm around Doris's waist.

Now, Doris thought, she just had to get home and send a text to her attorney to destroy those divorce papers. Though Frederick would be on probation until the Paris thing actually happened.

"I sold four of mine," Pauline said. "Well, three were a trinity set, a young doctor and his wife bought those. They were still arguing over if the paintings were going in his lobby or their house when they left."

"And who bought your other one?" Ruthie asked, finding happiness in everyone's success.

"My sister. Of course, I offered to give it to her, but she said, then it wouldn't be real art if I was giving it away. She insisted on the full price Daniel put on it and even asked for another set of the trinity in different colors for a house she was helping her friend decorate. Isn't that amazing? And oh yeah, my mother wanted one for her room. She has always been a sucker for our stuff."

Ruthie said she sold one of hers, and her daughters wanted the other two. Well, actually, Juliet really wanted one, and Natasha then had to have one.

"Your daughters. How nice," Carolyn said.

"How did you do, Carolyn?" Ruthie asked.

"Well," Carolyn said, reaching for her husband's hand, "Charlie and I have bigger news than my paintings."

Everyone grew attentive.

"We are going to have a baby!" Carolyn said and then broke into tears. Charlie couldn't stop his emotions from boiling over into tears himself.

"We didn't think we would ever be able to have a baby. This is truly a miracle," Carolyn said.

The women converged on Carolyn with hugs and excitement.

"If it's a girl," Carolyn said, "I want to name her Jill. Because since the moment Daniel told us about his wife, I have felt differently. I have thought about her a lot, and"—she paused and wiped her face—"I love that name."

Daniel blinked and nodded.

"Who would have dreamed that we, just look at us," Eleanor said, "would all be standing here together talking of selling our paintings as if we actually knew what we were doing?"

"And who would have dreamed," Elizabeth said, "that God has winked at us all?"

"Amen," Daniel said.